Blood Soaked

Gemini

By: Dillon Shafer

~
Born to fight, trained to kill,
ready to die, but never will
~

1

    The television explodes with noise as the crowd at the world championships goes wild. Seven-year-old Cassius wanders into the living room, rubbing his eyes, and dragging a stuffed animal in the shape of a monkey. His mother jumps up off the couch with a rushed comment to her husband, who stops their evening entertainment and powers down the screen before his son can see. Cassius' mother turns the boy around and sends him down the hall away from the living room, swaying her hips, and humming as she conveys her son back to the quiet darkness of his room. A few moments later, she returns and kisses her husband on the forehead. She drops into his lap and reaches out for the television remote. There is a moment of frightened scrabbling when she loses her balance, but then she regains her perch and the television is turned back on and their show continues, albeit at a slightly lower volume.

    The punch that had been frozen midflight connects with a stubbly pale face. The wiry man connected to the stubbly face crumples under the titanic blow. Blood sprays from the pale man's face as he hits the stained white floor. A giant of a man with the beard of a Cossack and the muscled body of a bear looms over the man, and puts his massive foot on the smaller man's throat. The smaller man grabs the behemoth foot with both hands and rotates it so that the bigger man lands on his back with a bang that rattles the cage surrounding the ring. The smaller man wraps himself around the large man's arm like a snake, and tries to wrench it from the socket, but the bigger man gets a grip on the little one's shoulder, and starts to slam him into the ground. Again, and again, the smaller man is pounded into the mat until he finally loses his grip on the larger man's arm. The bigger man takes this opportunity to grab the small man by the throat and hurl him at the chain link fence. The slight dark-haired man hits the mat and curls into a ball; he rolls into the rubber coated chain links of the cage and bounces off, rolling in a new direction. The big man lumbers to his feet and shakes his head, sweat flies from his bald scalp and his beard swings back and forth, he takes two steps and kicks the curled man as though he where a football. A loud crunching sound is followed by the clang of the cage as the little man hits the fence and falls on the mat. He makes no effort to move or defend himself as the mountain of tanned muscle strides across the ring and kneels next to him. Two fingers the texture of metal touch the small man's neck. Finding a pulse, the giant stoops and grabs the unconscious man's ankles. Spinning the man like an Olympic hammer toss, the giant lofts the man into the air and over the cage. Half a second later, a wet sounding crunch elicits a single scream from the crowd before it erupts in a euphoric roar. The giant stands in the middle of the ring. His arms raised over his head, his hands displaying a signature salute. Gnarled fingers curled into a tiger's paw, thumbs reaching across to touch his pinkies.

The cage begins to slide down into the edges of the ring and a walkway extends out from the edge of the stands. A bald black man in a charcoal grey suit walks out into the ring, he reaches out a hand and the giant grasps it in his. The black man taps a pin in his coat lapel and his voice booms out across the stadium, "That was spectacular! What do you think?" the crowd explodes again, just as loud as before.

"Once again Greg 'The Giant' Ivanov has shown us how a real champion defends his belt. What will you do now that you have defended your world title for the twelfth time?"

Greg leans down to speak to both the announcer and the microphone on his shirt. "I continue training; The Giant is champion, The Giant always champion."

"Thank you, Greg, I can't wait to see what you do to the next poor sap to climb the mountain. This is Charlie White, and this is goodnight folks." Charlie takes a bow with The Giant and a theme tune starts.

The television is shut off in Cassius' parent's living room, and the two adults sleepily shuffle down the hall, hand in hand towards bed. On the way, they both stop to peek in on Cassius. Under chain-link pattern sheets, with a poster of Greg 'The Giant' watching over him, the little boy is fast asleep. His parents smile and walk to their room, in here the bare corrugated steel walls of their home show the truth of their existence. These steel homes spread out for miles. Surrounding the major fighting arenas are entire cities built on the entertainment of millions.

Back in the arena, The Giant steps out of the showers with a towel wrapped around his waist, steam rises from the big man's skin and water drips from his beard. A young girl, no older than ten is standing on a bench with a towel in one hand and a comb in the other. The Giant sits on the bench and regards the man in military garb standing at attention across from him. "You have come again to ask me to train your special forces, no?"

"Yes sir, I am here as an ambassador of the English government, my employers would like you to instruct the SAS in London for the next three weeks, as there will not be another championship fight this month. You will be handsomely recompensed for your time." The soldier stands still while the girl who was standing on the bench towel dries The Giant's torso, arms, and head. The girl passes the giant his shirt, a tarp of blood red silk, which he slides on and begins to button up. The girl jumps down off the bench and begins to comb The Giant's beard. When she is finished, she walks back to a black and gold duffle bag and pulls out a pair of briefs and long black dress pants. She hands them to Greg as he addresses the man in the suit again.

"There will be no championship fight for at least four months, if you need me to train your little men I will need two months. And my rate will be discussed with the defense commandant." The Giant stands, and before he can drop his towel to finish getting dressed the ambassador salutes and hurries out of the change room. The Giant reaches out his hand to the little girl and she passes him a thick leather belt with a replica of the world championship buckle. "Why did you let that man in here while I showered?" Greg asks the little girl, she passes him a pair of large wraparound sunglasses as she answers. The sunglasses have been designed to conceal the bruising that has already started to rise around the giant's left eye.

"I knew your response coupled with your imposing physique would produce the effect you like to have on such men. I also knew that your unperturbed dressing habits would also keep the conversation timely, which you also prefer." The girl packs the towels and Greg's trunks into the duffle, then helps her father wrap his hands to hide the bruises and swelling. She then slings the duffle over her shoulder after slipping into a light blue sundress that covers the tank top and shorts underneath. Greg 'The Giant' and his daughter step out of the change room and into the press of bodies outside, each with a microphone or a camera. The Giant parts the sea of bodies effortlessly, standing at least a foot taller than anyone in the room; he walks towards the exit and the car waiting outside. As he reaches the car and opens the door, his daughter turns to the crowd of reporters.

"My daddy's The Giant, the greatest fighter to ever live, no one will ever defeat him." With that, she turns and hops into the car, slamming the door behind her. When the car is out on the street, father and daughter share a knowing glance. Greg extends a fist and his daughter meets it, her little hand about a fourth the size of her father's.

The next morning at four hours after midnight, Cassius's house is woken by the sound of his father's alarm clock. Cassius climbs out of bed and tidies his sheets, takes off his pajamas and stuffs them under a pillow. There is a race at school next week, and Cassius intends to take first place or die trying. He has already completed five rounds of his room, each marked by a thump on the steel wall by the door, by the time his mother comes to get him for a breakfast of toast, porridge, milk, and a raw egg.

After breakfast, Cassius's father leaves for work. He is a cook in the kitchens at the stadium, there is a local area tournament starting tonight so he will not be home until late. After his father has left, Cassius continues his training. His mother helps him count twenty push-ups, twenty sit-ups and thirty laps up and down the longest hallway they can find. After that Cassius's mother gives her son a hug, then feeds him a protein bar and gives him a bagged lunch.

Cassius arrives at school early he locks his lunch away in his desk then goes out to the yard to wait for the bell. He sits on a bench and watches the other children play on a climbing structure; a group of older boys walks up quietly behind Cassius and grabs the back of the bench. They all pull at once and topple the bench, Cassius falls backwards and rolls off the bench. He rolls into a crouching position and the boys circle around him, as Cassius comes to his feet the bell rings and the older boys disperse.

During class Cassius can only think about the looks on the faces of the older boys, he knew they would come back, they always did. But his mother's warnings ran through his mind as well.

"Don't get into fights at school, Cas." His mother always said, "Not unless you are sure you can win. You never know who might be watching. You are at that age now when people will be looking at you, sizing you up, looking to turn you into a fighter."

After the first block of classes, the students pour out into the yard. This time Cassius leans against a wall. When the group of six boys materialize out of the crowd Cassius is ready. He takes two steps away from the wall. The boys surround Cassius and the tallest boy steps forward. As the area around the boys clears a tenser energy permeates the crowd of children the taller boy leans over Cassius and growls down at him.

"A piece of tin can trash like you has no place here. Go die in a gutter!" Then the boy punches Cassius in the face. His head snaps back and he feels blood pooling in his nose. Cassius takes a deep breath to call for a teacher. However, he sees the camera mounted on the corner of the school building. At that moment everything goes silent, except for the pounding of his heart, after two near deafening concussive beats, Cassius moves instinctively.

Cassius exhales through his nose, spraying blood at the boy who punched him. Without looking, he lashes a kick out at his assailant's knee. The boy's knee snaps backwards and he crumples to his good knee. The boy behind Cassius takes a step forward; Cassius slams his elbow into that boy's throat and he drops to the ground, grabbing at his throat trying to take a breath. Turning his attention back to the first boy, Cassius unleashes a flurry of punches into the boy's stomach; ending with a single uppercut, rotating his entire body to knock the boy's head back. When the biggest boy's head hits the concrete one of the boys on Cassius' right swings at him. Cassius grabs the boy's wrist and neck using the larger boy's momentum to throw the boy at the three on his left knocking them all to the ground. The two remaining boys run at Cassius, as they swing Cassius ducks and rolls throwing both boys off balance. Cassius jumps up behind the two boys, and with a handful of hair in each hand Cassius Slams their heads into the concrete. Sickening cracks resound through the silent play yard. Cassius climbs to his feet, looks at the camera mounted on the corner of the school, and crosses his wrists under his chin.

Cassius walks into the front office and up to the desk, his shoulders barely clearing the top edge. The secretary looks down at Cassius with a smile. "Hi there Cas –" she stumbles over her own politeness as she sees the blood streaming down Cassius's face. "What happened? Are you okay honey? I'll call the nurse!"

Cassius looks up to the secretary, "I'll be fine Ms. Demarco. Could you take me to the principal's office? And can you please get a copy of the last five minutes' footage from the camera over the bike racks.

The secretaries face goes pale and she ushers Cassius into the principal's office. The principal looks down his long nose at Cassius, "What is it now Ms. Demarco? Why are you disrupting my noon time tea with this bloodied child?"

"Headmaster sir, there are six boys from the upper classes unconscious or in excessive pain out in the yard." Cassius says calmly. He takes a seat in front of the headmaster's desk, pinching the bridge of his nose to stop the bleeding.

The headmaster drops his tea, the cup shatters on the desk. The secretary turns to rush from the room, but she collides with a big man with salt and pepper hair as he walks into the headmaster's office. "Mister McAlister, how good to see you, I'm glad to see you have everything under control." He walks in and extends a meaty hand to Cassius "You must be Cassius, I saw your work on my way in, you have skill, great skill and promise. I am Igor Sovolar."

"You were the National Champion, until three years ago when you retired after dispatching Muhammad Avila." Cassius shakes Igor's hand vigorously. "I tried not to kill any of the boys out there, but the second one and last two might be in trouble."

McAlister's jaw drops "How are you two so okay with this? This boy just beat down four boys, unsolicited no doubt."

At that moment, the secretary rushes back in with a disk in her hand. Igor takes the disk, producing a mobile disk reader from an inside jacket pocket, slips the small disk into the receptacle on the side. As Igor slides into the second chair in the small office a small screen flickers to life. The footage starts just in time to see the circle start to form around Cassius. With each hit Igor becomes increasingly engrossed in the footage. When Cassius drops the largest of the boys, a slight smirk flashes across Igor's face; and when Cassius salutes the camera, he almost smiles.

"Where did you learn to fight, boy?" Igor rises from his chair and tosses the disk to headmaster McAlister. "You will find he never struck unprovoked. Send the boy home and I will be in touch with his family."

Igor walks out of the office and the headmaster points at the door "Out!" he screams "Out, you little monster!" Cassius leaves the office, and retrieves his things from his desk. He strides out through the yard and the students part around him.

When Cassius arrives home his mother rushes to the door. "Why are you home so early baby?" She cups her son's face in her hands, she instantly sees the flecks of blood under his nose and the slight swelling of his hands. "What happened to you? Did you get in a fight? Did anyone see you fight?" Cassius's mother hustles him into the kitchen and grabs ice packs out of the freezer. She puts one on the back of each of Cassius's hands and a damp towel full of ice on his face.

Cassius knocks the ice pack off his face and looks at his mother, "The fight was caught on tape, and a man said he would be coming by later today." Cassius' mother spins around, and her jaw drops, so does the cup of water she is holding.

Cassius looks up with a smile, "I won."

Cassius's mother kisses him so hard on the nose it starts leaking blood again and he cries out, then she rushes for the phone. She dials the arena and asks her husband to come home.

An hour later, Cassius's father comes home with a big man with salt and pepper hair. Cassius' father hugs his wife and introduces her to Igor. They go and sit on the couch in the living room. Cassius walks into the living room and his mother immediately scoops him up into her lap.

Igor introduces himself and asks to use the family's television. Cassius's parents agree and Igor plugs in his mobile disk reader. The television comes to life with the footage from the schoolyard camera. "Your son got in a fight at school today; this is footage from a camera in the school yard." Igor plays the footage, pointing out how every time Cassius so much as touches any of the other boys, they had swung at him first. Igor stops the video after the boy who hit Cassius goes down "Did you see that? That was the move used by The Giant in his second most recent championship defense." Igor resumes the video, and then stops it again just as Cassius stands up after knocking out the final two boys, "That is a variation on the winning move of last week's National championship fight. Your son is showing real talent and great promise, but he will need more than just talent and ferocity if he's going to become a world champion. I would like to train him to be that world champion." Cassius' parents look at one another in shock, as Igor continues, "Of course you would be given credit and compensation."

Cassius's father stands up and takes his wife's hand, "Can we have a few moments to think about this?" Igor tells them he will be back in the morning for their answer. After Igor has left their home,

Cassius' parents retreat to their room and close the door. While his parents are talking in their room, Cassius is in his room packing. By the time his parents emerge from their room, Cassius has all his treasures packed into a backpack under his bed.

The rest of the night goes by in a tense silence, until the end of the evening meal when Cassius' father makes an announcement. "Cassius, your mother and I have decided to let you go with Igor and train to fight. You will be leaving with him tomorrow morning after breakfast. I need to go back to work for the match tonight, but we will see each other tomorrow morning. Your mother and I are so proud of you." As his father finishes his statement, Cassius jumps to his feet and hugs both his parents, shouts a thank you and runs for his room. Climbing onto his headboard, Cassius carefully pulls down his poster of Greg 'The Giant' and rolls it up.

The next morning Igor and a man in a suit arrive at Cassius's home. The man in the suit passes Cassius' parents a heavy envelope, then picks up the backpack Cassius had packed the night before. When the man in the suit has left, Cassius's parents open the envelope and sign the papers within. Then they pass them to Igor, who gives them a second envelope. Igor extends his hand to Cassius, who hugs his parents one last time before walking out the door with Igor. Once Cassius has left, his parents open the envelope Igor gave them. Inside, there is a banker's note for one million dollars.

2

When the car pulls up to the sprawling mansion, The Giant opens his door and pulls his duffle bag onto his shoulder. He walks around and opens the other car door for his daughter. The little girl hops out of the car and runs for the front door. Her blue dress flaps in a light breeze. As she turns to smile at her father, a housekeeper opens the door to a mansion that sprawls in a field of training structures. Glass double doors open onto a dazzling marble and steel reception hall, polished stone and metal gleaming.

The little girl spins in a circle in the middle of the hall, shoes squeaking on the marble under her feet. The chandelier above her head sparkles with the light of a hundred tiny bulbs. Her father walks into the house without having to duck under the door frame. He hands his duffle bag to a slim, wiry teenage boy. He then walks through the hall and enters a stainless-steel kitchen and gives a two-fingered salute to a portly man in a white chef's coat. The portly man bows low, his tall white hat topples from his head and he catches it before it hits the floor.

"Welcome home Herr Ivanov, the kitchen is prepped and ready for your breakfast, the usual?"

Greg smirks, "Yes, the usual fare. Also, you will need to pack a bag for a few months. This will not be a problem, yes?"

The chef straightens up with a smirk. "No problem in the least, Herr Ivanov. Where are you travelling this time?"

The Giant walks around the kitchen, pulls a knife from a block and inspects it closely. "We will be traveling to London in two weeks to train the English special forces. You will have a sufficient staff to prepare meals for those I am training."

"Of course, Herr Ivanov." The chef bows again as Greg walks from the kitchen.

Greg is met out in the hall by a tall, thin young woman in black jeans and a tee shirt sporting a logo like the top of a white maid's apron. "Hello Daria, anything to report from last night?"

"No sir, all was well last night. How long will you be going away for?" Daria is momentarily distracted as she snatches a fly out of the air.

"How does everyone know that I am going out of town?" Greg asks as he unbuttons the cuffs of his dress shirt.

"Lady Viktoriya sent a message on your way home. She seems to be growing nicely into the role of a manager. Will she be going with you on this trip or shall I be looking after her here until you return?" Daria rolls her wrist over and a small holographic screen appears above her forearm.

"Vik will not be coming with me, but the two of you will not be staying in this giant house by yourselves." Greg pulls a small pad from his pocket, taps at it a few times, and then swipes up on the screen. A page of information appears on Daria's hologram.

"I am to take her to a training center? I thought you did not want her in a cage." Daria looks at the bearded man with curiosity.

"I have seen her trying to train in the yard when she thinks I am not looking. I cannot forbid her from fighting, it would be hypocritical of me. Take her to Igor, he hasn't taken another female student since you, but I think he will make an exception. He will train her, or break her will to fight; and if she breaks then she was not meant to fight in the first place." Greg tosses the small screen across the hall and it lands on a small wooden table by the door to the kitchen. "Please make yourself ready." Greg climbs the stairs to the second floor and walks to his room.

The Giant opens the door of his room and is met by a blast of cool air. He enters the room and pulls off his dress shirt, pale scars crisscross his entire body, and the bandages wrapped around his hands are stained with rusty splotches. He turns to look at the large bed in the center of the room, a furry mound in the center of the bed wriggles a bit. Then a lupine face covered in golden hair emerges. As big bright golden eyes focus on Greg, two floppy ears perk up and a long pink tongue lolls out in a canine smile.

"Hello Gladii, keeping the place secure as usual I see." The giant smiles as he tosses his crimson dress shirt onto the edge of the bed and walks into his closet. A few moments later he emerges with a silver hard case suitcase in one hand and a tight muscle shirt in the other. Gladii hops off the bed as Greg pulls the shirt over his head. As the two walk down the stairs to the main floor they are intercepted by an irate Vik.

"What's this I hear about you planning to ditch your manager when you travel to England tomorrow?" Viktoriya is standing in the middle of the stairs. She has changed into a pair of dark jeans and a purple shirt. Standing two steps below her father and Gladii, the difference between her high and that of her father is even more accentuated; however, Gladii still moves to hide behind Greg's legs.

"You haven't mentioned the good part yet." Greg smirks

"What good part?" Viktoriya cocks her head to one side, still frowning.

"I am sending you to train under Master Igor. He usually only takes boys, but he made an exception for his favorite student." The giant rests a slab like hand on his daughter's head and musses her hair, then he slips past her. Gladii slides past as well, keeping Greg between himself and Viktoriya.

Vik spins around on the stairs and gapes at her father, "Are you serious? You've always said I wasn't allowed to fight!"

The giant doesn't turn back to her, "Serious as a broken femur, now go pack or Daria will leave without you."

Viktoriya spins back around and dashes up the stairs to her room. She ducks under her bed and pulls out a dark blue shoe box. Inside are the sleek black and grey training clothes she had bought without her father's knowledge, or so she thought. After Viktoria packed her bags she raced down the large staircase and into the kitchen.

Greg looks up to see his little girl charge into the kitchen and grab a handful of mixed nuts. She slams the entire handful into her mouth at once and reaches for a bottle of water. Greg swallows his mouthful of eggs and laughs, "You don't have to hurry quite that hard dear, you have time for a proper meal..." He points at a plate of eggs and sausages across the table from himself, "Or should I just feed this to Gladii before I send him with you?"

Vik's eyes go wide with terror and she runs to the table and jumps into the seat in front of the eggs before the golden-haired dog can even get out from under the table. With titanic effort, Vik swallows her mouthful of nuts and scowls at her father. "Eggs give Gladii gas; I refuse to travel in a small car with a seventy-pound, hair-covered, spittle-dripping gas bomb."

Gladii lets out an offended wine from under the table. Vik just looks down at the dog, sticks out her tongue and makes a farting sound. She then proceeds to shove a whole fried egg into her mouth.

"I thought you didn't like it when I called you gopher girl." Daria leans against the door into the kitchen with a glass coffee mug in her hand. The deep, black liquid looks like it only stopped boiling a few moments ago, water vapors still rising thickly from the mug. Viktoriya glares at the tall redhead with all the fury her little frame can muster.

"If you keep going like that, your face will stick that way." Daria sips her coffee, and exhales steam.

Viktoriya gulps down the egg, still scowling at Daria "Even if it does stick I'll still be prettier than you." Vik stabs another egg and shovels the whole thing into her mouth.

"Come at me, Shrimpy." Daria tilts her head to either side, making her neck pop and crack.

"Ladies, please." Greg sits up and puts his hands in the air, "There isn't even this much hostility in a cage fight!"

Both women look at Greg with murder in their eyes. They look at each other and burst out laughing; Viktoriya doubles over and almost topples out of her chair. The giant looks from Vik to Daria, then back to Vik. A smirk crawls across his face then he joins the two girls with a deep hearty laugh.

After breakfast, Greg pulls Daria aside and whispers in her ear, "Look, I know you haven't spoken to Igor since your retirement. But he has reached out to me several times, he wants to make things right. Please, just give him a chance for old times?" Daria nods silently and turns away from Greg.

Daria, Viktoriya, and Gladii walk out of the front doors of the mansion and toward a low, sleek black sedan. A tall, dark skinned man in a black suit steps out of the driver's side of the sedan and tosses the keys to Daria. The toss is not very good and the keys fall short. Without breaking her stride Daria kicks the keys up into her hand before they can hit the pavement. Viktoriya loads her bags into the boot of the sedan and climbs into the front passenger's seat. Daria slides into the driver's seat beside Vik and engages the engine.

3

Cassius looks out the window of Igor's hired car as they drive out of the shanty town of shipping containers, knowing he will never return to this place. He turns away from the window to study the man who just bought him.

Igor Sovolar is a big man, with the frame of a man who was heavily muscled in his youth. His salt and pepper hair brushes the shoulders of his ash grey suit. His nose is prominent and aquiline, but it has been broken several times and reset poorly at least once. His gnarled and callused hands are folded in his lap, his piercing blue eyes close as if in contemplation.

"How much do you know about your new life Cas?" Igor's eyes are still closed.

"My name is Cassius, Cassius Slade. Don't call me 'Cas'." Cassius wrinkles his nose at the nickname.

"I own you, boy, if I want to call you Sally you will respond to such." Igor reaches across and cuffs Cassius across the back of the head.

Cassius leans against the door of the car, rubbing the back of his head, "Yes, sir."

Igor sits back on his side of the car, "The rules are simple, respect me or fear me, either way, my job is to turn you into a human weapon. If I fail, you die. So, you must trust me not to fail you. Can you do that?

"I will try, sir." Cassius turns to look at Igor again, there is kindness in the old man's eyes, nothing soft, nothing gentle, but kindness none the less.

Igor and Cassius travel in silence for several hours. When the car stops Igor does not move to get out, he just opens his eyes and pops his neck. Then he turns to Cassius, the boy regards him with expectation. "Your second lesson boy, diet is more important than training in a fighter's regime. For the near future, you will be intaking calories and nutrients every two hours. Once you are in the fight circuit you will go down to larger meals, five times a day." Igor moves his hand and rolls down his window. The man in the suit, who had been driving the car, passes two paper bags in through the window. The smell of grilled red meat hits Cassius like a hammer. Igor passes the smaller of the two bags to Cassius. "Eat everything put in front of you at meal times. Asking for more is acceptable, but everything you get, you eat."

Cassius opens the bag and his heart stops. In the bag is a beautifully laid out salad covered with a boiled egg, ham, and cheese. Cassius pulls the salad out of the bag and finds a fork in the bottom of the bag. Cassius digs in to the salad with the gusto of the hungry, stressed seven-year-old he is; meanwhile, Igor pulls a greasy, paper wrapped burger from his bag and begins to eat. As Igor watches Cassius devour his food, Igor starts to remember another scrawny, awkward slum boy he took in over twenty years ago.

When Viktoriya and Daria arrive at their destination, they are greeted by a tall dark skinned blonde boy of about fifteen. He bows deeply and introduces himself, "Welcome to New Thrace, Training camp for the champions of Igor Sovolar, or should I say champion." He looks up with a self-assured grin. "My name is Garrick Steel-bender. How can I help you?"

Daria bows to Garrick and smirks, "Garrick North, scouted from a tin-town in Egypt. I was unaware you had gained a title. Who coined that one?" Daria looks back to the boy in time to see him blush. "Alright Steel-bender, I have come for a meeting with master Igor. Is he here?"

Garrick glances at Vik before turning his attention back to Daria. "Master Igor is not here at the moment. He is on his way back from a scouting trip however, and will be here within the hour. If you would like I can find you two a seat and maybe something to eat?"

"Something to eat would be excellent, thank you. We will require one on circuit serving, as well as one off circuit serving." Daria picks up her bag and slings it over her shoulder, and nods for Vik to do the same. As they walk up the path towards the main house, a sleek blue classic sedan with deeply tinted windows rolls into the semicircular driveway. Vik and Daria stop to watch the car roll towards the house. Gladii pops his head out of the back window of Daria's sedan and lets out a solitary bark, then ducks back inside. This gets Garrick's attention and he turns back as well.

When the car rolls to a stop the driver climbs out. His pale face half obscured by a large pair of driving glasses. The driver walks around to the rear door and opens it. Igor slides out of the car and pulls himself to his full height, his spine snaps and pops in protest and he groans. Garrick slides past Daria and Vik, heading for the back of the car to collect his master's luggage. When Igor sees Daria and Viktoriya he smiles, then he sniffs the air and turns towards Daria's car. Igor strides to the rear door of the black sedan and opens it; Gladii pours himself out of the car and sits on the pavement, his tongue lolls out of the side of his snout as he smiles at Igor.

"Gladii! How's it going boy? Did you watch over these two lovely ladies? Who's a good boy?" Igor squats down and pets the big golden dog vigorously.

During this exchange Cassius climbs out of the other car. His eyes wide with wonder as he takes in the vast training fields and the large main house. Vik sees him and scowls, but Cassius doesn't notice.

The boy Vik sees clamber out of the car after Igor Sovolar is a thin, wiry boy. His hair is a deep brown and hangs long, framing a round bronze face. He's cute, for a little kid; but Viktoria senses something else, something she doesn't like. She glares at the boy, trying to figure out where she had felt that feeling before.

"He's cute." Daria leans down to whisper in Vik's ear. "He has killer instincts too. Look at how he holds himself, even when he is gawking at his surroundings. Poor thing, must be his first time outside of whatever tin-town Igor found him in." Vik glowers up at Daria.

Igor straighten up from petting Gladii and turns back to the assembled group of fighters "Viper, I see you are doing well." Igor bows to Daria, then he turns to Vik, "You must be Viktoriya. I have heard high praise from your father." Igor bows more shallowly to Viktoriya, then he turns to Garrick, "Carry those bags in boy, then show Cassius to his room, eighteen should suffice. Then come see me in my office." Igor turns back to Daria and Viktoriya and smiles wide.

"Come, we have much to discuss. Let me show you around the compound."

Igor leads Daria and Vik up the path towards the house. leaving Cassius and Garrick in the care of the tall, pale driver. Cassius turns to speak to Garrick, but just as he opens his mouth the other boy speaks.

"Hey, I'm Garrick North, I've been training under master Igor for almost eight years. If you're here, that means the master sees something special in you. How did you get scouted?" Cassius looks up at the bronze skinned boy, he is smiling with a genuine friendliness Cassius had not seen very often in his life.

"School yard fight, I took down six kids at least a year older than me. What got you here?" Cassius smirks up at Garrick and slings his backpack over his shoulder.

Garrick laughs, "Not the popular kid in school, huh? My moment was when I took down three adults in an alley. Master happened to be walking by and saw me fight." Garrick lifts Igor's bags and starts to walk towards the main house. Garrick leads Cassius through a large, elegant entry hall and through a door mounted in the side of a large central staircase.

Cassius walks through the door behind Garrick and looks down the long, carpeted hallway; doors at twelve-foot intervals are emblazoned with bronze numbers. Garrick walks past four sets of opposing doors. He stops in front of a door with a bronze number plaque nailed to the door which reads "eighteen". Garrick turns to Cassius and knocks on the door behind him.

"These will be your rooms until master Igor says otherwise, mine are at twenty-six." He points down the hall to the door four doors down from Cassius's rooms. "I'm going to have someone bring you your next meal, you are on the off-circuit diet, right?"

"Yes, I am. Wait I have 'rooms', like, of my own?" Cassius looks stunned, staring at the door behind Garrick.

"Well it's only the illusion of privacy down here," Garrick kicks the door behind him and it swing open. "The doors don't even latch down here." He steps to the side to let Cassius into the room. "Hey, I never caught your name." Garrick extends his hand to Cassius.

Cassius reaches out and clasps the taller boys forearm, "My name is Cassius, Cassius Slade." Garrick turns and walks farther down the hall, still carrying Igor's luggage.

"Well met Cassius, well met." As he disappears around a corner, Cassius turns to go into his rooms.

His rooms, the thought was still unbelievable. Cassius simply spent time wandering between the three small rooms. Half the space is taken up by a room occupied by a couch and coffee table on one side, a round table surrounded by chairs in the other. A large feather bed occupies most of the small bedroom. Lastly, his own bathroom, this door latches with a small metal hook. Just as Cassius settles onto his couch there is a knock at the door. Cassius jumps up and moves to open the door, but just as he gets to it, the door opens. A tall blonde woman in a pair of jeans and a seafoam green blouse step into the room carrying a grey plastic tray.

"Hello, my name is Elizabeth Sovolar. You get to call me El, just like the rest of the fighters. It is my job to make sure you are in fighting form, so that essentially puts me in charge of every aspect of your life when you are not training. Igor breaks you, then I put you back together so you can do it all again." El sets the tray down on Cassius's table. In the tray, there are scissors, a razor, and a tape measure, along with several other, smaller implements. "This also means you can ask me any questions you may have."

"Ok, first question then: do you have to cut my hair?" Cassius eyes the scissors suspiciously as El circles around behind him.

"As long as you know the risks of hair as long as yours." El grabs a handful of Cassius's hair and rips his head back, she smashes her elbow into Cassius's face and lets the boy drop to the ground. "Long hair might make you pretty, but it becomes a target for your opponents." El bends back down and picks Cassius up by his shoulder length brown hair. She drills her knee into Cassius's stomach; she tosses him onto the couch and walks back towards the tray. El picks up a pair of long, sharp scissors and inspects their edges. "So, do you still want your hair that long?"

As she turns back around she sees Cassius roll off the couch, he lands in a crouch with one hand planted in front of him, his hair cascades in front of his face. When he looks up, blood is starting to dribble from his nose. "I want to keep my hair."

He lets out a primal growl and El pulls a chair out from the table and sits down. She pulls off a pair of horn-rimmed glasses and hooks them in the low buttoned front of her blouse. "I think I'm going like you, kid. Alright then, any other questions?"

"I have so many questions." Cassius walks over to the table and climbs into a chair.

"Should I start with the general orientation while you eat?" As El finishes her question, there is a knock on the door. A young boy in a white chef's coat enters the room with a steel tray. He sets the tray in front of Cassius. Cassius nods as he digs into a plate of steamed vegetables and scrambled eggs. El relaxes into her chair and pulls a small pad out of her back pocket.

"So, you obviously know why you are here. Igor thinks he can train you to be a great fighter, and that's the first thing, you aren't training to be a contender or a crowd pleaser. You are being trained to be a champion." El leans over Cassius's tray and snatches one of the round blueberries from a bowl and pops it in her mouth, "since you are on an off-circuit diet, you will take a lot of meals here in your rooms. However, the meals at six in the morning, eleven, and six at night will be taken in the main hall with the other trainees and trainers. You will have a trainer personally assigned to work with you every day. Once a week you and your trainer will have a training session with Igor." El steals another blueberry and continues reading from her notes. "Once a month, you will spar with the other off circuit trainees. I have an office at the end of this hall in room zero. If you need anything, don't hesitate to ask."

Cassius looks up from his clean plate, "I get a personal trainer? When do I meet them?"

El smiles, "You will meet your trainer tomorrow, after the morning group meal. Make sure you are up. Get one of the other boys to show you where to go. You already met Garrick, I'll let him know to look out for you until you get your trainer." El stands up and takes the tape measure off her tray. "Now, I need your measurements for your new clothes."

4

Viktoriya follows Master Igor into the entrance hall of the main house and up the central staircase, at the top are a pair of large stained-glass doors. Igor pushes though the doors to reveal an elegantly appointed office. The furnishings are constructed of sleek, polished steel and dark glass. Daria drops into a steel chair and kicks her heels up onto Igor's desk. Viktoriya takes the second chair on the close side of the desk, she rests her elbows on her knees and clasps her hands, she looks up at Igor as he walks behind his desk.

Igor pauses behind his desk, his arms clasped behind his back. He looks up at a framed photo of his younger self, a towel thrown over one shoulder. Above Igor in the picture, Vik's father, Greg is comfortably resting his elbow on Igor's head. He has the world champion title belt resting on his shoulder, and even though his face is a bloody mess, both men are absolutely beaming.

"That was the night your father won his first world championship." Igor turns to the two women and sits in the chair on his side of the desk.

Daria rolls a knife out of her sleeve and begins cleaning her nails. "Greg said you would be willing to train Vik here. If it were up to me she would be training under Daedrana, or Naomi; someone who actually has experience training female fighters."

Igor leans over his desk and pinches the bridge of his nose, rubbing the habitual pressure points of a long-time glasses wearer. "Viper, who trained you to fight?"

Daria snaps the small knife back down her sleeve and glares at Igor, "You trained me to fight."

"Yes, and look how you turned out!" Igor gestures to Daria, as if showing Daria her own body.

"Look at me indeed!" Daria shoots up out of her chair. She peels her jacket off and tosses it over the chair back. She steps back from the chair, grabbing the V-neck of her shirt. "During my last tile defense, my opponent caught me in an unfamiliar hold." As Daria turns away from Igor and Viktoriya, her shoulder muscles bunch and her shirt tears away. "It was a variant on the backbreaker throw I was taught." Daria moves her blood-red hair aside to reveal a thick, pale scar running from the nape of her neck to the small of her back. Dispersed at seemingly random intervals, smaller scars trail off the main scar like tree roots. "Thinking she had missed her set up, I swept her legs out from under her. The drop fractured half of the vertebrae in my upper spine." Daria turns back to Igor and Vik; she flips her hair back over her shoulder and pulls a pen knife from the pocket of her jeans. "Needless to say, she was startled when I stood up and put my foot though her face." Daria opens the pen knife and cuts a line in her flesh over her ribs, just below the band of her sports bra. "I can hardly feel anything above my waist. I can't taste anything unless it is an extreme of flavor or temperature." Daria flicks her wrist and the blood-soaked blade buries itself in Igor's desk. "That backbreaker drop is taught in every women's training academy, because it requires less brute force than the throw you had me spend hours practicing!" Daria looks at Vik, whose mouth is hanging open. "So, yes, I have a problem with you learning to fight at a men's academy." Daria throws her coat back over her shoulders and turns to leave the room.

Igor stands from his desk and calls after her, "Don't you think that was why Greg sent you?" Daria spins on her heel and glowers at Igor, he clears his throat and continues. "Greg and I were there the night Nora broke your back. After you passed out Greg climbed over the cage to carry you out. He almost missed Viktoriya's mother going into labor making sure you had the best care."

Daria looks at Igor, tilting her head in confusion. "Get to the point, Igor."

Igor clears his throat and wraps his knuckles on the desk. "I know I made mistakes with you. That's why I haven't taken on another female student since. I want to try and make things right between us." Igor slides a desk drawer open and rummages for a second. "I have the facilities and staff to train eighty fighters. However, right now I only have thirty-five boys here. Thirty-six if you count the new boy, Cassius." Igor steps around the desk and tosses something to Daria, who snatches it out of the air with the speed of the lightning fast serpent she is named for. "I'm not as young as I was when I trained you and Greg, Daria." Igor pulls a pocket watch from his vest and looks at the picture fitted into the cover. "My daughter Elizabeth was never really a fighter, she trained here and under Naomi. But, she has never been in a real ring. She has no real idea of the pressure these boys will experience, when the cage is locked and the person across from them is out for their life. We do, and that's a bond you can't put into words."

"Igor, this still isn't making sense to me." Daria looks down to see what Igor had thrown at her. A small, silver key rests in the palm of her hand, attached to the key is a golden skull keychain, along with a paper tag with a string of numbers.

"I am going away for a while, I hope I can leave this place in your capable hands. I will send my girl Elizabeth up here to help you get settled." Igor walks past Daria and grabs the handle of one of the tall stained-glass doors. "You once trusted me enough to pick your fights. I guess the question now is, do you still trust me?" Igor pushes though the door and lets it close behind him.

Viktoriya turns around in her chair to stare at Daria. "So… I guess that means you are in charge now?"

Daria looks from the key in her hand, to the doors, then to the elegantly appointed desk. Then she bursts through the stained-glass door and shouts after Igor, who is already at the bottom of the stairs and heading towards the front door. His driver is standing just inside with a large suitcase at his feet. He hands Igor a small attaché case and lifts the larger case.

"Hey! Old Man!" Daria shouts from the top of the stairs, her arms planted on her hips. Igor turns to look up at her. Daria smiles massively "Don't expect your things to still be in my office when you get back."

Igor laughs, setting down his case he salutes Daria with a stance he hasn't taken in decades. He crosses his forearms and spreads his fingers so his hands are split down the center.

Daria beams and salutes back. Raising both hands to shoulder height and crooking her first two fingers of each to mimic snake fangs.

As Igor turns to leave a young boy in a white chef's jacket scurries into the main hall from a side door and rushes up the stairs to Daria, his balance is impressive. He is carrying two plates; one appears to be the final resting place of an entire chicken coop, the other holds a small portion of scrambled eggs and a few strips of bacon. Pinched between the two plates is a basket filled with fresh berries. Daria opens the stained-glass door behind her and the boy rushes into the room, he sets the three dishes down on the desk and pulls two sets of utensils out of a pouch in his apron. He then quickly retreats down the stairs, presumably towards the kitchens.

Daria walks back across the office and eyes the overstuffed leather armchair behind the desk, with only a slight hesitation she drops into the chair. She then proceeds to put up her feet and drag the larger of the two plates onto her lap.

"So, what does this mean for my training?" Vik asks between inhuman sized mouthfuls of egg, bacon, or berries.

"Everything is about to get very interesting." Daria looks at the antique style desk phone - that would have to go – and finds the name Elizabeth on one of the speed dial presets. "Very, very interesting." Daria hits the button next to the name on the phone and spears a piece of chicken breast with a fork.

When Elizabeth arrives, Daria and Viktoriya have just finished their meals. The tall blonde closes the door behind herself and steps into the office. She looks over at Daria sitting behind the desk and nods. "So, Dad finally managed to get you behind that desk, huh Daria?"

"Beth, long time no see." Daria kicks her feet down off the desk and stands up.

"The fighters call me El now." Elizabeth walks into the room and leans against the back of the other chair. She extends her hand to Viktoriya and the young girl takes it. "You must be Viktoriya, Greg's girl."

"Are you going to be training me?" Viktoriya jumps out of her chair and sets her plate on the corner of the desk.

El laughs and covers her mouth with one hand. "No, that won't be me. I'm in charge of the wellness of the fighters and trainers. I have found you an ideal trainer, all the trainers here were either regional champions or trained to fight here themselves."

"Who is it?" Viktoriya is practically bouncing with anticipation.

"Her name is Nataliya, she was a regional women's champion for four seasons before she retired for a job here." El flicks her wrist and her holographic wrist unit winks to life. She taps a few keys then looks back to Vik, "She should be here soon to help get you settled. Daria and I have a few things to discuss if she is going to be running this place."

Vik picks up her suitcase and moves closer to the door. In a few moments, there is a knock on the office doors and a slender woman in her mid-twenties steps inside. She flicks a lock of brightly colored hair from her face and extends her arm to Vik, who grasps the taller woman's forearm in a fighter's greeting. Natalya bows to Daria and El, then picks up Vik's suitcase and leads the young girl out of the room.

When the door closes, Elizabeth and Daria share a look, Daria comes out from behind the desk as the door softly clicks shut. A few taps at El's wrist unit and there is another click from the door. A set of magnetic locks engage, ensuring their privacy.

"Why did you really leave?" Elizabeth asks Daria, her sapphire blue eyes boring into Daria's emerald green.

"I couldn't fight, hell I couldn't even walk for over a year. What good would it have done to mope around here like a lame horse?" Daria looks away, not meeting El's gaze.

"Maybe I wasn't clear enough with my query. Why did you leave *me*?" Elizabeth's voice waivers, she clenches her fist and her nails bite I into her palm.

"I couldn't feel anything!" Daria slams her fist on the desk, her knuckles clip the edge of a stone carving, stripping the flesh from the backs of her hand. "I still can't, not for the most part. I don't just mean physically either, the injury didn't just break my body, it broke something more important too." She looks at her torn skin and exposed bone.

Elizabeth steps forward and takes Daria's mangled hand gently in her own. "How did you get the rest of your body back?" El reaches into her back pocket and opens a small med kit. She pulls two small aerosol vials out of the case and sides it back into her pocket.

"Months of agonizing rehab. Reminded me that if there is enough of it, I can still feel pain." Daria holds her hand still while Elizabeth sprays an antiseptic on her torn skin, followed by a skin-tone matching adhesive bandage.

"Then let's consider this the start of your next phase of rehab." Elizabeth wraps her arms around Daria. "I missed you Daria."

Daria pulls Elizabeth close to her. Even though she can barely feel the other woman pressed against her, memories she thought she had buried rushed to the surface. "You were right." Daria whispers in El's ear, "This hurts just as much as rehab." Tears well up in Daria's eyes, as she holds on to Elizabeth. "I missed you too, Beth."

5

The next morning, Cassius leaps out of his bed to a high-pitched whining sound. The moment his feet touch the floor beside his bed, a holographic clock appears on the wall across the room from him. An electronic voice chirps at him.

"the time is zero-five-thirty, you have thirty minutes before group breakfast."

Cassius rushes into the main front-most of his three small rooms, there are a pair of dark grey pants and a red shirt tossed over one of the chairs in the dining area. Cassius grabs them then rushes to clean up. He gets outside his rooms with five minutes to spare. Garrick is waiting in the hall, leaning against the doorframe of suite seventeen.

"Morning sleeping beauty. Guess El didn't get to cut your hair, huh?" Garrick cantilevers himself off the door frame and drapes an arm over Cassius's shoulders. Garrick's arm is clammy against the back of Cassius's neck, and not from a shower. "You got to sleep in kid, my trainer had me up and running laps an hour ago." At that moment, a stocky girl in in a slate grey track suit pokes her head around a corner farther up the hall, she scowls at Garrick.

"Steel-bender, why are you not doing the exercise I assigned you?" the woman in the track suit strides around the corner, her chestnut brown bob cut swaying with each step. "Who is this?" the woman, obviously Garrick's trainer, gestures at Cassius.

"This is the new kid, Cassius. El wanted me to show him to the dining hall to meet his trainer." Garrick gives his trainer a roguish smile, which is clearly not wasted. She smiles back and nods her head in the direction she came from.

"Run along then, don't want you to have to rush your first meal on hell day." Still smiling, she turns and strides back up the hall. Cassius looks up at Garrick, who's good looks are now soured by the slightly green tinge of his skin.

"Let's go." Garrick starts to walk down the hall, Cassius hurries along behind.

The dining hall is half full, pairs of people eat meals side by side on benches at long tables. Garrick waves to someone and turns to Cassius, "Your trainer is named Devi, he's the one in the jeans and purple shirt heading this way. Good luck."

Garrick turns and jogs over to take a seat on the bench next to his trainer. Cassius looks towards Devi; the man looks to be in his mid-thirties and built like a grappler. Red hair bristles from the lower half of his face, contrasting with his shiny, bald head. He extends a hand the size of a bear paw to Cassius. "You must be Cassius. I am Devirian, I'll be your trainer here."

Cassius clasps the big man's hand and smiles up at him. "So, I've been told you are in charge of breaking me on a daily basis?"

Devirian laughs, "Is that what El told you our job is?" He gestures to a spot at the table where two plates have been set out with fresh greens and a piece of pink something Cassius has never seen before. "My job is to work with my fighter, in this case you, and set up a training schedule that works with your strengths. That way, we can make you into the best possible fighter you can be."

Cassius climbs over the bench and inspects the strange thing on his plate. "What is this? Or what was this?" Cassius pokes at the piece of meat with a fork and it flakes off in sheets of soft pink stuff.

Devi stabs one of the pink sheets off his own plate and puts it in his mouth. "That's salmon. It is a kind of fish." Cassius's eyes go wide as he stares at the piece of fish.

"I thought you couldn't get fish anymore." Cassius tentatively puts a small piece in his mouth. The flavor of sharp lemon bites through an undertone of salt water. Cassius shovels a large fork full of the fish into his mouth and smiles with delight.

"Good, isn't it? Master Sovolar was able to get his hands on a live breeding pair of the creatures about twenty years ago. They are a great source of protein and high in healthy oils." Devi puts the last piece of the salmon in his mouth and watches Cassius eat. "Any way, today we will be reviewing the fight that got you scouted. There is digital footage, so it will be easier than some of the fighters here. From there I will try and discover what style of fighting suits you best."

Cassius looks up at his new trainer and tries to ask, "Styles of fighting?" but his mouth is full of fish so it comes out garbled. Devi laughs and cups his hand over his ear.

"Sorry, I didn't quite catch that. Don't talk with your mouth that full." Devirian takes a sip from a metal mug and clears his throat.

Cassius gulps down his mouthful of fish and sips water from a pewter mug. "I said: 'what are the styles of fighting?'"

Devi takes another sip from his mug and takes a deep breath. "There are several distinctive styles a fighter can train in, they usually focus on one particular type of move, holds, strikes, throws, and so on. It is my job to determine what your strengths are so that by the end of the week we have a good idea what direction to focus your training in. Master Sovolar was a striker, and bigger guys like myself are usually trained as grapplers. You are still developing, so your attitude has more to do with your style than your body type."

Cassius takes a moment to look around the room again. There is a balcony he hadn't noticed before. Leaning on the railing, watching the pairs of fighters and trainers, is the woman Cassius had seen in front of the house yesterday. He nudges Devirian and nods towards the balcony. "What makes her such a guest of honor?"

"That's Viper, the only female fighter Master Sovolar ever trained. I've heard that she might be taking over the academy soon." Devi stands up and takes his mug, "Come on, kid. Let's go review the footage of your fight." Cassius looks at his plate and mug, then at Devi's plate. He stands up and takes his mug with him. Devi ties his mug to a loop on his belt, Cassius looks down at his own belt. There are two loose leather ties in his belt, Cassius pulls on them and ties his pewter mug to his belt.

Devirian leads Cassius though the labyrinthine stone halls to a white room with two rows of chairs. Devi flips his wrist and a holographic screen appears over the inside of his wrist. He taps a few keys and a wall section drops away to reveal a large screen. A few more key taps and the screen comes to life with the camera view of

Cassius's old school yard. Devi points to a seat in the first row, and Cassius drops into the chair.

Before Devirian can start the video, the door bursts open and Elizabeth walks into the room and waves at Devi. She sits down next to Cassius and gives him a thumbs-up. Daria strides in hot on Elizabeth's heels. She looks at Devi, who bows slightly.

"Devi, I'm curious about this new fighter. Is this a tape of him fighting?" Daria leans against the wall beside the door.

"Yes, Master Viper." Devi bows again and hits another key on his wrist unit and the recording begins to play.

Devi smirks as Cassius flips his third opponent over his shoulders and into three other opponents. El claps when Cassius drop-slams the last two opponents into the asphalt.

When Cassius salutes the camera, Daria signals Devirian to pause the playback, she turns to Cassius and speaks for the first time since the recording started. "You have no style. You used a mix of both grappler and striker styles, but your movement is better suited to a breaker style. Devi, meet me in Igor's office to discuss Cassius's training routine." Daria walks out of the viewing room. El jumps up and rushes after Daria.

6

Elizabeth rushes down the hallway to catch up with Daria, "Viper! Hold up. A word, if I may?" Daria slows her pace and allows El to catch up.

"If it's about that boy you can save your breath, I saw it." Daria snaps at Elizabeth, she runs her fingers through her long red hair and sighs.

"I haven't seen anyone move like that in years, not untrained at least." Elizabeth flicks her wrist and her wrist unit winks on.

"I need information on that boy's parents, teachers, anyone who could have taught him how to fight like that." Daria keeps walking down the hall. El follows close behind rapidly tapping at keys in her wrist unit.

"I'll have Cassius's file sent to your desk unit as well as anything I can dig up, I need something a little more powerful than my wrist unit for that. I am going to get my desk unit. I'll meet you back in your office in five minutes?" Elizabeth turns a corner and jogs down a hallway that leads back to the fighter's rooms.

Daria arrives in her office. The photos have been taken down and the old phone removed, but the sleek steel and black glass furniture remain. Daria sweeps behind her desk and calls up the screen for her desk unit. The slim metal case projects a holographic screen covered with all the information she has on the new boy, Cassius Slade.

Elizabeth bursts through the office door carrying her own desk unit under her arm. She sets it down across the desk from Daria and calls up the screen.

"Find anything?" El asks as she pours over constantly changing lines of text. "I'm trying to get into the boy's school records, but the legal work hasn't gone through yet. So, I'm having to use a back door. It takes a little longer than the proper channels but, in this case, we can't wait for the paperwork." At that moment, there is a knock on the door and Devirian pokes his head in.

"Get in here and close the door." Daria snaps at him, he steps inside and Daria presses key on the side of her screen, the magnetic locks engage and the room is sealed.

"What's going on?" Devi walks up to the desk and takes the empty seat next to El. "What did you two see that has you so wigged out?"

Elizabeth turns her screen to Devi and replays a small portion of Cassius's fight. Devi stares at the screen as Cassius flows through the first three strikes of the fight. "look at his feet, the way he transitions between strikes. What do you see?"

"He moves like he knows what he's doing. I don't think I see what you want me to see…" Devi stare at the screen a while longer, watching the looped video, trying to discern what the two women want him so see in his new pupil.

After a few moments, El breathes an exasperated sigh and pauses the video. "He fights like a girl." She walks Devirian through the video, pointing out all the variations Cassius made to his movements. "It may just be because these boys are all stronger and bigger than he is. However, we suspect he has had some level of training. We are searching his records to see if anyone he spent time with was a former fighter or trainer."

"Got something." Daria makes a sweeping motion on her screen and an identification page winks up on El's desk unit. "I didn't recognize the name because she used a pseudonym when she fought. She also changed her name when she got married, but this is definitely the person who taught him to fight." The photo on the screen is a shoulder up shot of a young woman, electric blue hair cascades over her pale, freckled face.

"That's Dawn Stryker, wasn't there a huge scandal around her a few years ago?" El starts to scroll through the fighter registry, looking for more info.

Daria leans back in her chair, "She was a regional champion for about five seasons. Then she entered the National Championship ladder. I remember because I was the National champion at the time. I had my eye on her. Her style was a mix of striker, grappler, and…"

"Breaker style, like Cassius, right. I have her record here, originally from the tin-town around New-Yuma. She was the youngest women's regional champion, only sixteen. During her national champion bid, she had a relationship with a chef from the tin-town around the arena. She got pregnant, it cost almost all her earning to pay off her contract. She fell of the map at that point."

"What was the chef's last name?" Devirian is leaning forward now trying to read El's screen.

"Last name, Dallas. That isn't the interesting thing though." Elizabeth pulls her glasses down her nose and squints at the screen. "Can you find a better scan of her ID with her maiden name?"

Daria makes another swiping motion and a photograph of a fighter's license card appears on Elizabeth screen on top of her other readings. "Dawn Stryker, a.k.a. Suzan Dallas. Formerly named Suzan Slade."

Devi leans back in his chair and whistles a low note, "What are the odds, huh? The son of a disgraced fighter gets scouted, and the name he uses to register is Slade. Not as obvious as Stryker, but still an homage to his mother's legacy."

"Devirian, I might have to give this boy to another trainer. Would you be alright with that?" Elizabeth turns to Devi and clasps her hands in her lap.

"I'm willing to share the training of this kid with someone else if you want. But I want to be in on this. I'm the best Grappler you have here, I defended my title against strikers and breakers before I retired. I have insights and experience you can use." Devi sits up a little straighter and looks Daria in the eyes. "Use me, Master Viper. I can help you make this boy a champion."

Daria smiles at the young, freckle-faced girl smirking from her screen. "El, do we have any trainers who fought like Dawn?"

"I'll have a look. I know we have several female trainers who were strikers. But that combination is rather unique." Elizabeth shuts down her desk unit and turns to Devirian. "Go do a simple cardio session with the boy, I will have a training team assembled in two hours."

Devi nods and stands up, he heads towards the door, then pauses and turns around. "So, what is your plan with Cass? Are you going to train him to adapt his style to work with his body, or train his body to fit his style?"

"I know what happens when you train your body to a style no one else uses. You take people by surprise, but it can leave you blind to variants you have never trained for. That's where you come in. We are going to train him to use his style the way it was originated, your job will be to prepare him to fight male style variants." Daria hits a key on her screen and the stained-glass doors behind Devirian unlock. "Two hours Python, we look forward to your insights."

Once Devi has left the room, Elizabeth stands and tucks her desk unit under arm and turns to Daria. "You trained as a striker and a breaker. You could train this boy better than anyone here."

"I was never very good at teaching." Daria stands from her desk and looks out the windows at the training field. Pairs of fighters and trainers run laps, obstacle courses, and lift weights.

"You taught me a lot." El steps up beside Daria and takes her hand.

Daria smiles "That was different and you know it." She squeezes El's hand and leans her head on the other woman's shoulder. "I still have no clue what I'm doing, Beth."

"That's why I'm here, to help you figure it out." Elizabeth lets Daria lean on her shoulder as they watch the bustling activity in the yard below.

Viktoriya's chest heaves, her lungs burn, and her heart thunders in her ears. She crosses the line on the track and collapses to her knees. Natalya stands over her with a stop watch running on her wrist unit. She stops the timer and records the time in a notes section.

"Get up." Natalya growls at Vik. "Your lap times are terrible. Go get a drink and meet me at the weights."

Vik crawls on her hands and knees to the edge of the track, then she climbs to her feet and stumbles over to a wooden barrel. The water inside is cool and still as glass, Vik resists the urge to dunk her head in. She unlaces a pewter mug from her belt and scoops it full of water. She gulps downs the crystal-clear water, rivulets run down the sides of her mouth and spill onto her grey tank top.

Natalya has already walked over to the weight training section of the yard. As Viktoriya jogs to towards her, Natalya lifts several kettlebells off their racks and sets them on the grass in pairs.

"Watch me, do as I do." Natalya steps in between two matching kettlebells, she crouches down and picks them up. Then she lifts the weights out from her body until her arms are parallel with the ground. "Hold here for five seconds. Then lower them back down and move to the next set." She sets the weights back down on the ground and steps back.

Viktoriya manages to get through three increasingly heavy pairs of weights before a muscle in her left shoulder cramps and she is pulled to the ground. Natalya seems impressed and she makes a note in her wrist unit. Natalya reaches down and helps Vik to her feet. "Well done, let's have a look at that shoulder." Natalya spins Vik around and drives the pad of her thumb into the still cramping muscle in Viktoriya's shoulder.

Vik lets out a short high-pitched cry, if Natalya hadn't been holding her up she would have collapsed again. In a moment, however, the pain in her shoulder is completely gone. She turns around as Natalya releases her, she looks up at the woman with multi-colored hair and musters a scowl.

"How did you do that?" Vik rotates her shoulder in a slow circle. "My shoulder is fine now."

"I was trained as a disrupter. I was taught to focus on pressure points and cramp my opponent's muscles. I learned pretty quick how to stop cramps as well as instigate them." Natalya smiles, "Just remember that I can make you run laps with low grade leg cramps if you are difficult."

Vik laughs uncomfortably, "So, what's next master Shocker?"

Natalya bursts out laughing, "Oh, that's good, 'Master Shocker' I like it!" Natalya throws her arm around Vik. "Want to go watch the other new kid kill himself in the obstacle course?" Natalya leads Vik over to where a crowd has gathered around the wood and steel obstacle course. Vik finds an unoccupied view of the course and her jaw drops.

Natalya's estimate is accurate. Cassius, the young boy she saw climb out of Igor Sovolar's car yesterday morning is halfway up a wooden climbing wall. This puts him a well over six feet in the air. As

Vik's jaw falls open, Cassius makes it to the top of the fifteen-foot wall and looks down the other side.

Cassius inspects the downward side of the wall, the face is sheer, it was designed to be jumped from. Cassius looks out at the crowd of fighters and trainers. Some of them are smirking at him wryly. Cassius turns to the back side of the wall, there are three ropes that are hanging from a beam above his head down to the ground. Cassius grabs one of the ropes and starts to pull it up. Once he has gathered the rope up to the top of the wall, Cassius salutes the watching crowd and kicks the rope down the smooth side of the wall. There is a cheer from the watching crowd as Cassius jumps off the top of the wall. He catches the rope halfway down the wall and slides the rest of the way to the ground.

The rest of the obstacles are relatively easy, a barbed wire crawl, followed by a set of low fences. Viktoriya moves to the end of the course and extends her fore arm to Cassius in a fighter's greeting. Cassius reaches out and grasps her forearm. "I'm Vik. You are the kid from yesterday, right?"

Cassius smiles at Vik and pulls a chunk of mud out of his long, dark hair. "I'm Cassius. Yeah, I only got here yesterday."

"Why did you take on the intermediate level course?" Vik looks back over the course, intimidating obstacles stretch for an acre of muddy ground. There are multiple ways though the course, each route designed for a different fighting style.

"Had to show I'm not weak." Cassius tosses a chunk of white chalk to Vik. "Where I'm from, if you aren't hard, you are prey. I spent too long as prey." Vik catches the lump of chalk and stares at Cassius. He smiles and nods towards the course, "I took the route I thought was hardest."

"Great. I have to do this now too, you realize that?" Vik scowls at Cassius and makes her way to the start of the course. A crowd forms instantly as she walks through the one-way rotating gate at the start of the course. Vik looks at the lump of chalk in her hand, then looks at her first choice of obstacles. There is a white calk mark above a hole at the top of a ramp, Vik smirks as she steps onto the ramp. As she puts her weight on the ramp the surface under her foot slides back. Viktoriya grits her teeth and dashes up the ramp, there is a gap between the end of the ramp and the wall with the chalk mark. Vik launches herself from the end of the ramp and manages to get her head, arms, and shoulders through the long rectangular hole in the wall. She pulls herself through onto a raised platform and smiles.

Vik follows the white chalk marks, completing ever obstacle. By the last few obstacles sweat is pouring down Vik's back under her shirt. She looks up at the fifteen-foot wall she had seen Cassius climb, there is a white chalk mark on the timber suspended above the top platform. Viktoriya grabs one of the two ropes hanging from the beam and starts to climb. At the top of the wall, Vik collapses on her back and coughs. She struggles to her feet and makes the decent down the other side of the wall. She completes the barbed wire crawl with ease. When she gets to the set of four low walls, Viktoriya climbs on top of the wall. Bunching every muscle in her body, Vik leaps from the top of the wall and clears the second, landing in the mud between the second and third walls. Vik climbs up over the third wall and vaults over the fourth. She walks up to the end of the course and hits a large green button. The section in front of the button slides open and Viktoriya walks out of the obstacle course. Cassius walks over and offers her his arm, just like she did before. She grabs Cassius's forearm and smiles.

"That was fun. They decided how to train you yet?" Cassius hooks his thumbs into his belt as he and Vik walk towards a water barrel.

"I don't think so, but my trainer is a disrupter. So maybe they have. What about you?" Vik unties her mug and scoops up water, she gulps down the whole cupful.

"Not yet. I feel like they would tell you if they decided to train you that way." Cassius unties his own mug and scoops it full, he takes a sip and clears his throat. "As far as I know, no disrupter has made it any higher than a regional title. Then again, I just learned there were such things as disrupters or sabers, so I'm hardly an expert."

Vik laughs, "You are right though, disrupters need to maintain focus and accuracy. Which can be pretty hard when you are getting thrown around by a grappler, or eating a constant barrage of fists from a striker."

"You two seem to be making friends." Cassius and Vik spin around, Daria is leaning against one of the lamp posts that surround the running track. "Cassius, Vik. Come with me." Daria turns around and starts to walk back towards the main house. Vik looks at Cassius then jogs after Daria. Cassius looks from Daria, to Vik, then to his half full mug. Cassius dumps the contents of his mug out over his shoulder then starts to jog after Viktoriya.

Daria pushes through the door of her office, followed closely by Vik and Cassius. Three trainers are leaning against the various walls of Daria's office. Daria leans against her desk and nods to each of the trainers in turn.

"Larina, regional champion for four seasons. Trained and fought as a striker." A thin woman in a leather jacket cantilevers herself off the wall and steps towards Vik and Cassius.

"Cassius, you know Devirian. National champion for five seasons, Grappler." Devi salutes Cassius and Vik.

"Nalia, Regional champion for five seasons. Fought as a breaker and a student of slide style." A dark-skinned woman with tightly braided blonde hair steps forward and crosses her arms.

"These three will be working together to train both of you." Daria flicks her wrist and her wrist unit winks to life, she hits a few keys on the device. There is a series of chimes as all three of the trainers receive an information packet. "You have access to all information on both pedigrees, as well as information on the style we are replicating. I'm moving these two into rooms one and two, you will have full liberty with their schedules. The weekly check ins will continue as usual, as well as the monthly sparring. However, these two need to learn by doing, and we need as much documentation as possible. We are trying to start a new multitype school here, no room for messing around."

Viktoriya clears her throat, "Will someone please tell me what is going on?" she lightly lifts her foot to stamp it, then promptly thinks better of it when Cassius steps forward.

Daria holds her finger up to silence Cassius and he stops, his gaping mouth sliding slowly shut again. "We know your secret kid. Don't worry, we want to help you with your plan." She taps a few more keys on her wrist unit and her desk unit screen opens and grows to the size of a large television screen. A video of a cage match starts to play. "The one with blue hair is Dawn Stryker, this is footage from her last regional title defense against Tanya."

The camera follows the two women as they fight, exchanging parried blow after parried blow. Suddenly, Dawn lets one of her opponent's strikes past her guard. With a grin, Tanya commits fully to the strike. At that moment, Dawn twists her torso. She lightly taps Tanya's right elbow, redirecting her fist wide of Dawn's torso. Dawn grabs Tanya's wrist in one hand, and takes a handful of blonde hair in the other. Using the Tanya's momentum, Dawn slams her opponent into the mat. Still holding on to Tanya's wrist, Dawn kicks Tanya's shoulder with her left foot; the impact of the kick tears Tanya's shoulder out of its socket. Dawn bends down and checks Tanya for a pulse. Finding one, she pulls Tanya's head up by her hair. Dawn flicks her wrist quickly left, then right, and a deep crunch comes from Tanya's neck.

Daria stops the recording and closes the screen. "There are several more recorded fights on your desk units. Study them as much as you need to. You are dismissed."

Nalia nods and walks out of the office, her flowing grace a testament to her training in slide style. Devi walks up to Cassius and pats him on the shoulder, he smiles at Vik before leading Cassius out of the room and down to the fighter's quarters. He walks right past room eighteen and continues down the hall to room one. Devirian pushes the door open and steps inside, Cassius follows him in and looks around. The poster he put up on the wall in his other room is hanging on the wall in the same place.

"Okay, question time." Devi is sitting on the couch and pats the seat beside him. Cassius walks over and drops onto the couch. "I'm sure you have lots of them."

"Only a few." Cassius looks up at Devi, his trainer is listening intently. "How did you find out about my mom?"

"Master Viper saw it in your fight recording. Your mom taught you how to fight." Devi looks at the boy beside him, he doesn't share either his mother's skin tone or eyes. The hair however, it's a dead ringer.

"She always told me not to fight at school." Cassius looks down at his hands. "But she couldn't help teaching me."

Devi flicks his wrist and the holographic screen winks on. "Cassius did you ever see her fight?"

Cassius looks back up at Devi. "Not before today."

Devi smiles and hits a key on his wrist unit. "Want to watch more? I have to study these recordings anyway." A holographic screen winks into existence over the coffee table.

"That would be good, thank you." Cassius sits back on the couch and settles in to watch his mother take people apart with her unique mixture of styles.

Viktoriya follows Larina down the fighter's quarters hall. When they arrive at room two, Larina opens the door and steps inside. Viktoriya is hot on her heels. Vik stops just inside the door and clears her throat.

"Okay, I have a few questions." Starts to pace in the dining area. "Why are we learning a style of a fighter who never made it beyond regional champion?"

Larina flops onto the couch on the far side of the room. "Dawn's combination of styles was never used before she used it. More importantly, it's been fourteen years since her first match and no one has ever replicated it." Larina opens the screen of her wrist unit and pulls up the holographic screen over the coffee table. "Which means, either this will be a total waste of time and Dawn was just a fluke, or this could be a style like Elba's combination of striker and grappler styles. A combination so effective, there are entire training academies dedicated to training it."

"I get that, I guess." Vik keeps pacing. "Next question. I know my pedigree is my dad, The Giant, but who is Cassius's pedigree? He's a tin can kid."

"Cassius is Dawn's son." Larina smirks as Vik stops pacing and stares at her. "She had a kid and had to retire."

Vik comes over and sits on the couch next to Larina. "Are you going to watch more of her fights? Can I watch too?" Larina smirks and starts the recorded fight.

After Devirian leaves, Cassius moves to his new bedroom, under the edge of the bed right where it was in his last room is Cassius's backpack. After a moment of digging, Cassius pulls out a pair of navy blue, fingerless leather gloves. His hands are still far too small to fit the gloves, but he puts them on his hands anyway. The backs of the gloves have the stenciled initials 'D.S.' carved into the leather and highlighted with gold paint.

9

Several days go by, Cassius and Vik rise early every morning. They run, lift weights, and most importantly spar. Every day Cassius and Vik train new holds, strikes and throws. Two weeks after their arrival, Cassius and Vik meet their trainers at breakfast.

"Ready for your first chance to show off what you know?" Nalia sips a steaming cup of coffee and scoops scrambled eggs onto her fork.

"What?" Cassius and Vik both mumble around mouthfuls of eggs and ground meat.

"Today is sparring day. Everyone in your skill group will be gathering. You will be paired off and you will spar. It gives you some additional insights into fighting other styles." Devi smiles and sips water from his mug.

"We aren't allowed to have you fight to the death anymore." Larina smiles and punches Devi in the arm. "Remember when they had us fight to the death every three months?"

"Yeah, they ran out of kids a lot quicker then." Devi hides his smile behind his mug as Vik and Cassius pale and share a glance.

Cassius nods to Vik, and the two kids start shoveling food into their mouths at an even greater rate. Nalia guffaws and clutches her stomach. "Stop it, you two are making my stomach hurt just by looking at you."

Once Cassius and Vik finish their plates of food Nalia, Larina, and Devi lead the pair down a winding set of hallways. When they arrive at a row of steel doors, Larina turns to Viktoriya.

"Come with me, I'll help you fasten your padding this time." The two girls disappear though one of the doors and Devi signals to Cassius.

"We'll go through here." Devi turns back to Nalia and she nods.

"See you boys in there." Nalia turns and walks through one of the other doors.

Devirian leads Cassius through one of the steel doors. The room on the far side is a locker room lined with white metal lockers. Devi pulls open a locker and tosses a set of tight black garments and grey protective pads onto the central bench. Cassius changes into the new garments and Devi helps him into the Pads. Devi kneels in front of Cassius, he hands him a bronze ring. The outside of the ring is carved with wolves and lightning, looking inside Cassius sees several small barbs. "It's a hair ring." Devi takes the ring back and motions Cassius to turn around. Devi gathers Cassius's hair and slides the ring over it. Devi turns the ring and Cassius feels the ring pull at his hair. Devi turns Cassius back around and hands him a padded helmet.

Cassius feels up behind his head. The bronze ring has constricted around his hair, tying it securely. Cassius looks up at Devi "Thank you."

"Go get 'em kid." Devi leads Cassius to the other door on the far side of the room. "Oh, and kid." Devirian meets Cassius's eyes

"Don't kill anyone yet, okay?" Cassius smiles and walks down a short white-washed hallway.

Cassius approaches the door at the end of the hall and it slides open. As Cassius steps through the doorway his eyes dart around the space inside. A twelve-sided fighting ring dominates the room. Rubber coated chain-link fencing rises around the ring. Daria is standing in the center of the spring-loaded mat.

Cassius walks up a set of metal steps and walks to the center of the ring. Another door opens and Troy walks though. He looks at Cassius with smirk and climbs the stairs of the ring. Devi steps out of the shadows along the walls of the room and throws a latch on the outside of the cage locking it shut.

"Put your helmet on." Daria grimaces at Cassius and waits for him to strap his helmet on. Daria grabs each of the boy's right hands. "Don't kill each other, and no breaking bones. Dislocation is acceptable." Cassius and the Troy nod. Daria counts to three, then throws the boy's hands down and away.

Cassius steps back into a low crouch, his hands floating just under his chin. Troy is a grappler, and his height coupled with the addition heft of his big boned frame compliment that style perfectly. If Troy gets Cassius to the mat it's all over. Troy has adopted a medium stance, ready to redirect strikes into throws. Cassius can see the trap, and rushes right in.

Cassius feints an open palm strike to Troy's face; the larger boy moves to deflect the blow and grasps for Cassius's arm. Before Troy can find Cassius's wrist, Cassius drops to the mat and slides past troy on his knees. As he passes the taller boy Cassius plants his right hand on the mat, the leather of his padded gloves binds against the canvas redirecting his momentum. Cassius uses this change of direction to lift one of his legs and strike the back of Troy's knee. The blow knocks Troy off balance. He recovers quickly, however, he grabs the front of Cassius's chest padding and throws the smaller boy halfway across the ring. Cassius lands on his back and rolls to the far cage wall, he uses the cage to pull himself up. Troy rushes across the ring, hoping to ram Cassius against the cage. Cassius feigns instability until Troy is fully committed to his charge. Then Cassius jumps, he pulls on the cage and gets enough height to push himself off the cage and over Troy's head. Cassius lands behind Troy as he barrels into the cage. Cassius drives an elbow into Troy's back and gets a grip of his thumb, Cassius twists the digit brutally and Troy cries out. The larger boy falls to the mat as Cassius presses his advantage, locking the larger boy's thumb in a painful grip. Then a whistle sounds and Cassius relinquishes his hold on Troy's thumb. Daria walks over and helps Troy to his feet.

"Well fought boys." Daria sets a hand on each of the boy's shoulders in turn "Troy, Grappling is the art of controlling your opponent. If you allow anything to control you; anger, pain, or even a desire to make more of a spectacle, you lose that control. If you hadn't been focused on flattening Cassius against the cage you would have noticed he was faking." Troy nods and rubs the joints of his thumb. "Cassius, you are used to fighting untrained schoolyard toughs. You hesitate after a showy maneuver to see what effect it has. If you had followed up that leg sweep you pulled, instead of getting royally launched, you could have ended the fight much sooner." Devi reemerges from the sidelines and opens the other side of the cage. Both boys shake hands and walk down the stairs together. Devi leads then to rows of seats Cassius hadn't seen when he came in. The two boys take all their pads off and sit to watch the rest of the sparring matches.

Viktoriya is up next, her opponent is a slight boy with blonde hair. The boy is a striker and he rushes Vik in a flurry of knees and elbows. Vik takes up a defensive posture, she uses her hands to deflect the elbow strikes and her padded elbows stop the knee strikes in their tracks. By pressing the attack, the boy is making Vik react to his movements, limiting her ability to use any striker styles. Vik pulls back and leaves her leg out, drawing a kick to the knee any striker would be hard pressed to ignore. But the strike never comes, instead Vik's head snaps sideways from a brutal kick. Viktoriya spins with the impact, turning in a full circle before landing on her knees on the mat. Daria picks the whistle up off her chest, but before she can sound it to end the match Vik moves in a flurry. Grabbing the cage behind her head, Vik kicks out, both her heals connect with the boy's face and helmet and he goes down. Vik jackknifes herself to her feet and wipes glistening red blood from her lips. The boy rolls away and climbs to his feet, the two fighters circle for a moment then Vik throws a wide lefthanded punch. The boy's elbow snaps out and blocks the fist, just as Vik's leg connects with the side of the boy's knee. As her opponent falls to the mat Vik follows, dropping her elbow right in the center of the boy's chest padding. He gasps for air as Daria blows her whistle.

Vik stands up and offers the boy a hand up, he coughs and grabs her hand. Devi stands in front of the two fighters and regards each of them. "Viktoriya, you don't have enough experience to reliably draw attacks like that. Hugo, how's your nose? You need to learn a little bit of ground work before you start fighting."

Out in the yard, Cassius and Viktoriya lean against a water barrel. Cassius offers up his mug, "You did great in there."

"You didn't do bad yourself." Vik taps her mug against Cassius's.

"At least I didn't get kicked in the head." Cassius takes a sip of his water, and Viktoriya dumps her mug over his head. Cassius splutters as the water pours over his face.

10

The next six months pass much as before, Cassius and Vik get strong and faster. The day before the monthly sparring competitions, Vik and Cassius are in the yard doing strength training. Larina is spotting Cassius as he lifts a bench press bar. Viktoriya is doing kettlebell drills when she hears a deep bass voice.

"I think you can hold that a little longer, don't you?" Viktoriya drops the kettlebells to the ground and spins around.

"Dad!" Viktoriya runs over and hugs her father, she barely comes up to his waist. Cassius finishes his rep set and Larina helps him stow the bench press bar. He sits up on the bench and Vik waves him over. As Cassius approaches, Greg smiles at him and extends an inhumanly large hand in greeting.

"Cassius, this is my dad." Vik says as Cassius takes The Giant's hand.

"Greg Ivanov, an absolute pleasure to meet you sir." Cassius shakes the larger man's hand.

Vik and Cassius's trainers all gather around and shake Greg's hand. Even Devi, the tallest of the three barely comes to Greg's shoulder. Greg takes a step back and looks at his daughter, then he turns to the three trainers.

"So, what style has Igor chosen to have you three train my daughter?" Greg looks at the three in turn.

"Actually, Igor left almost two months ago. I'm in charge here now." Daria walks through the training yard towards the group. She walks right up to Greg gives him a hug, she leans up and whispers in Greg's ear. "We need to talk in private." When she pulls away she introduces the three trainers. "Cassius and Vik are training in a mixture of styles; striker, grappler, and breaker." Daria nods to each of the trainers as she lists their specialties.

"That's an unusual mix, usually you can pair grappler with striker or breaker. But breaker and striker don't usually harmonize." Greg strokes his impressive beard.

"As a student of both Grappler and striker, you know that grappling techniques are very transitional." Devi steps forward, he had been tasked with coming up with a response to this issue. The fact Greg is also a grappler gives the two men a common ground, making Devirian more confident in his delivery. "The trick is to use this inherent flux state to transition between striker and breaker moves. Nalia is also a student of slide style, the two of us have been working to increase the already highly transitional nature of grappler style to form a cohesive style."

At this point Nalia steps up to give her insights, but Greg holds up a hand. "Please spare me the full dissertation, at least until I have seen this system in action."

"Monthly trials are tomorrow morning. You will be staying the night, surely." Daria smiles at Greg "I will have a room made ready." Daria flicks on her wrist unit and taps a few keys.

While the adults are embroiled in conversation, Cassius nudges Vik and smirks. Vik nods and the two take a few steps back from the group, they start to stretch and Viktoriya tilts her head from side to side popping the joints in her neck. She extends her hands in loose fists and Cassius meets them, simultaneously starting the sparring session, and setting up the rules of their match. Light contact, minimal joint manipulation.

Cassius opens the fists exchange in a striker stance, arms up creating opportunities for both fist and elbow strikes. His legs are centered under him as he floats on the balls of his feet. Viktoriya takes the hybrid stance Devi and Larina had agreed on as the best position from which to employ grappler and breaker techniques.

Daria looks up from her wrist unit just in time to see Cassius open the match with a snap kick aimed at the side of Vik's head. Viper smirks as she sees Vik drop under the kick and strike the back of Cassius's leg, introducing more momentum than he had anticipated. "You wanted a demonstration of the style?" Daria nods towards the pair as they exchange metered strikes. "Looks like you are getting one." The whole group spins around to watch Cassius and Vik spar.

Cassius flows from the striker stance into a low-slung grappler stance. Vik baits a throw attempt, then grabs Cassius's wrist and pulls herself into a shoulder strike. The strike connects, but Cassius tanks the impact and sweeps her legs. Vik lands on the ground and rolls out of range as Cassius brings down an obviously delayed axe kick. Cassius changes his stance again, one hand is raised above his head like a fencer, and the other is dropped low as though to block a low kick. Cassius flips into an aerial cartwheel and both his feet clip lightly off

Viktoriya's high guard. Cassius drops to the ground and slashes a kick at Vik's knees again, but she jumps. Planting both her hands on Cassius's shoulders, Vik turns herself around and pushes off. She lands on one hand and one knee facing Cassius. Without looking back, Cassius springs off with his hands, launching himself feet first at Vik. Viktoriya falls to her back, as Cassius passes above her she plants both her feet in his stomach and pushes upwards. Cassius is propelled upwards, he rolls to the side and coughs. Vik steps over and rests her foot on Cassius's chest.

Greg claps, "Very impressive, well done Viktoriya." Greg hugs his daughter and turns back to Cassius. "Boy, a word?" Cassius nods and kips up off the ground. The two of them take a few steps away to a water barrel and Cassius unties his mug from his belt. "How long did you train under Master Igor before Viper came.?"

Cassius fills his mug from the barrel and looks up at the big man. "I got here with Master Igor shortly after Master Viper and Vik." Cassius drains the contents of his mug in two gulps.

"You obviously knew how to fight before you came here, then. Who taught you?"

Cassius looks down at his feet, the refills his mug. Greg strokes his beard and looks back to where his daughter stands surrounded by her trainers. They seem to be giving praise and advice to her. "Nevertheless, I need you to promise me something." Greg takes Cassius's mug from his hand and drains it.

"What could you need from me?" Cassius grimaces up at The Giant. The larger man hands Cassius back his mug.

"Don't go that easy on my daughter ever again." Cassius spits water from his mouth in a jet.

"What are you talking about?" Cassius look up at Greg.

"It was so obvious it was painful. You transitioned through styles in that sparring session to show the styles versatility. But you gave yourself away, not just the axe kick everyone saw that and thought you just didn't want to kick her in the face. Admirable, however the last stance you took was a combination of saber and slide styles. No one else caught it, but you just used five different fighting styles. Look kid, I've been around long enough to know that it's a good idea to keep some potential concealed. But, at least with my daughter, you should be completely open with your skills. Don't let those skills rust up, you hear me?"

Cassius nods, "I was going to tell them about it, but…"

"You know Dawn, don't you kid?" Greg leans in closer.

Cassius nods again "She is my mom. She's been teaching me how to fight since before I could walk."

Greg's eyebrows lift, "Interesting, anything we haven't seen yet?" Cassius stays silent, looking down at his feet. "Alright, let's get back to your trainers." Greg leans off the water barrel and starts to walk away when Cassius mutters something unintelligible. Greg turns back smiling, "What was that, kid? I didn't catch that."

Cassius looks up at Greg "I can fight disruptor style too." Greg's smile widens and he kneels in front of Cassius.

"Now that's one hell of a Pedigree." Greg pats Cassius on the shoulder and stands back up. "Come on, kid." Greg leads Cassius back to his trainers and addresses Daria. "You said you needed to talk to me?"

"Yes, follow me." Daria turns and signals Greg to follow her back to the main house.

When Greg and Daria reach her office, Daria closes the door and turns to The Giant. She snaps an open palm into the large man's stomach and grabs his beard to pull him down to her level. She hisses right in his face.

"Did you know Igor's plan was to leave this place to me?" Daria snarls and Greg tries to pull back.

"No, I didn't. He said something about wanting to finally make things right with you. I thought he just wanted to apologize. I had no idea he was going to bolt on you like that."

Daria releases Greg's beard and The Giant stands back up to his full height. "Was there anything else you wanted to talk about?" Greg looks around the office, there is a holographic screen open on the wall, names are paired off on one side and on the other is a list of unmatched names. Daria is still trying to pair her students off for the sparring tomorrow.

"Yes, actually there is something." Daria walks up to the holographic wall screen. "I want to offer you a job. I want you to retire your title and come work here."

"Where is this coming from?" Greg takes a step towards Daria.

Daria turns back around. You Aren't getting any younger Greg, you'll be thirty-two in a few months. You are the oldest world champion ever.

"I'm also only the third world champion, Daria. Neither of my predecessors retired, besides, I feel fine." Greg frowns at his friend. "Daria, are you alright?"

"I'm fine." Daria turns back to the half-finished sparring brackets. "Will you at least help me finish these fighting brackets?" Greg steps up behind Daria and looks at the unassigned names. Beside each name is a number and a letter, some of the fighters have two or more letters, while most have only one.

"Is 'S' saber or slide style?" Greg studies the board.

"Saber, we don't have any good sliders at this level."

Greg taps Cassius's name a card opens with a photo of the boy, basic biometrics, and his skill levels. Greg drags the tag to an open slot, then finds one of the boys with a similar score and places him opposing Cassius. "Kaden is a saber style, are you sure about that?" Daria looks at Greg.

"He may surprise you, he certainly did me." The giant sorts the rest of the brackets with ease. "What do you say we give these kids a taste of the ladder?" Greg hits a button on the screen and an elimination bracket system generates on the screen, along with computer generated predictions. Daria steps up beside The Giant.

"Excellent. Looks like fun."

"For you maybe. Remember the strain a ladder like this would put on us?" Greg grits his teeth.

"Sometimes the winner of the ladder couldn't fight the defending champ for a month or more." Daria looks at the computer predictions. "There are some unpleasant match ups in here." She points to one of the semifinal brackets. "A disrupter against a higher-level Slider? I feel bad for him."

"Probably won't happen though." Greg points at Cassius's bracket. "I'll put money on Cass making it to quarter finals, he back traces the bracket. Before he gets dropped by this Grappler, this boy is just too big for Cass to deal with."

Daria extends her hand, "I'll take that bet, I don't think he'll make it past the first match." The two old friends shake hands.

11

The next morning, Cassius makes his way into the dining hall and takes his seat next to Vik. Their trainers eat in silence and Cassius looks at each of them in turn. No one will meet his eyes, so he turns his attention to his food.

"What did I miss? Cassius looks around the dining room, every other trainer-fighter pair is either silent, or muttering to each other inaudibly. Other teams are conspicuously absent. Then Cassius sees the holographic screen mounted on the wall. The framework of an elimination ladder is highlighted, as Cassius looks around the room all the screens show the same ladder. Cassius steps up from the bench and walks to the wall. He studies the ladder, he finds his name placed against Kaden Blaine, a saber style fighter about his age. Cassius smirks, The Giant had something to do with this.

Cassius turns and walks back to his seat and drops down to finish his breakfast. Vik stares at him. "What?" Cassius looks up from his plate.

"What do you mean 'What?' You saw the board!" Vik's shouts echo in the dining hall.

"Yeah, and your point?" Cassius sips from his mug, "It's just an elimination ladder."

"Just an elimination ladder?" Devi looks Cassius right in the eyes. "Why are you so calm?"

"I can deal with Kaden." Cassius turns to Vik, "Think you can drop Troy this time? He planted you last time." Cassius smirks as Viktoriya glares at him.

"I'll make him tap out, easy." Vik turns her glare to her trainers, "This is just like any match. We can do this. Got any last-minute advice?"

Nalia leans over the table and starts murmuring that Viktoriya needs to press any advantage she can get, while Larina leans across to Cassius, instructing him in the best ways of using striking against a saber fighter.

When Cassius steps into the changing room, there is a rack along one of the walls. Replicas of bladed weapons hang from the rack. Cassius straps on his pads then moves to examine the rack of blades. The weapons are made of braided lengths of wicker wood, painted, and shaped into the forms of the most iconic bladed weapons of history. Cassius lifts a curved, single handed saber from the rack and swings it experimentally. Cassius thinks back to what Greg had told him yesterday.

"Don't let my skills rust up huh, old man?" Cassius swings the saber down to his side and walks down the hallway towards the ring.

Cassius's opponent is already in the ring. Kaden stands beside Daria as Cassius climbs the steel steps into the ring. Daria raises an eyebrow when she sees that Cassius has chosen a saber as well.

"You don't have to fight in his style you know." Daria looks down at Cassius with mild concern, but he just smiles.

"Just gives him a range advantage if I don't have one, at least at the beginning." Cassius rests the saber on his shoulder and turns to face Kaden.

Kaden nods to Cassius and pulls his padded helmet down onto his head. Daria grabs the tips of their sabers, counts to three, then starts the match. Kaden jumps backwards and sets himself up in a low left guard, body turned to present a smaller target.

Cassius mimics Kaden's guard, Kaden smirks. Kaden lets the tip of his saber drop to the right, then flicks it out and up, driving the point towards Cassius's face. Cassius throws a wide uppercut, catching Kaden's strike in the intricate guard that surrounds his hand. Cassius jabs in under Kaden's guard, he manages to grab Kaden around the throat. Cassius pushes off the ground and lifts Kaden into the air as he rises. Kaden's eyes widen is shock as he finds himself falling. Kaden slams into the mat and his saber falls from his hand and rolls across the mat. Cassius pulls himself up off the mat and throws his sabre at the cage wall. The blade of his saber passes through one of the gaps in the cages chain link. Cassius kips Kaden's saber into his hand and throws it into the opposite chain link section. Cassius hauls Kaden to his feet by his chest padding. Cassius looks at Daria and tilts his head questioningly.

Daria nods to Cassius. Cassius pulls Kaden forward then steps through the other boy, slamming his forearm into Kaden's chest. Kaden slams down so hard he bounces back up off the mat. Daria slides across the mat and taps Kaden on the chest, she holds her hand over the boy's mouth until she feels his breath. She taps the boy on the cheek and pulls him to his feet. The cage is opened and Daria leads Kaden out of the ring. Cassius stands in the center of the ring until Daria comes back up.

"What was that?" Daria squats in front of Cassius. "Where did that viciousness come from?"

"That's what this style is, at the core it is based around vicious efficiency." Cassius cracks his neck. "When's my next fight?"

Daria's eyes widen and she looks Cassius up and down. "We don't know who your opponent is. Next round will be in about an hour."

"Thank you, am I excused?" Cassius waits for Daria's nod before climbing out of the ring and exiting the room. In the hall, he finds Kaden sitting on a bench, his mug full of water in one hand. Cassius drops onto the bench and lightly smacks Kaden on the arm.

"Thanks." Kaden mutters into his cup.

"What for?" Cassius looks at him, confused.

"Thanks for not hitting me in the face. Kaden smiles, and Cassius notices that his nose and teeth are perfect. Cassius has taken more shots to the face in the last six months than he ever had before in his life. Yet, somehow this boy had not taken a hit.

"You need to learn something for when what happens next time." Cassius stands up from the bench and smiles at Kaden. "And learn to take a hit, man." Cassius turns away and walks down the hall, pulling off his helmet and gloves as he walks towards his rooms.

When Viktoriya comes out of her changing room she is the first one. She jogs up to the ring and takes up a spot beside Daria. The young girl looks up at the former champion, she smiles and gives the older woman two thumbs up. Troy walks out of one of the doors and climbs the steps into the ring. Daria sets the two opponents and starts the match.

Troy rushes at Viktoriya, just before impact, Vik leaps into the air. She gets her legs wrapped around Troy's neck, using the large boy's momentum Vik rotates her body and smashes Troy's face into the mat. Vik scrambles onto Troy's back, locking her legs around Troy's waist. As Troy tries to rise to his hands and knees, Viktoriya locks her feet in between Troy's legs. Vik leans back and starts to rain strikes down on the back of Troy's head. Troy fights to his feet and falls backwards, hoping to crush Vik between his mass and the mat. Vik feels the shift of momentum and slides down Troy's legs, as he starts to fall Vik hits the ground. Vik snaps her legs up off the mat and helps Troy to the mat with a double kick to the stomach. While Troy is dazed, Vik manages to climb to her feet. Vik steps between Troy's legs with her own left leg and wraps Troy's legs at shin level around her leg. Holding Troy's legs in place, Vik then grabs Troy's top leg and steps over him, flipping Troy over onto his stomach. She leans back and compresses Troy's lower back. Troy cries out and slams his hand into the mat. Daria calls the match and Viktoriya stands back up, releasing Troy's legs from the punishing hold she had set up. Troy rolls onto his back and cradles his crushed calves.

Daria helps Troy to his feet and he stumbles out of the ring. His trainer helps him down the stairs and out of the room. Daria looks down at Vik, "Your style is improving, good work on that submission. That won't win you any real matches though."

Vik smirks up as Daria, "He couldn't stand when I was done with him." Vik cracks her neck and pulls her helmet off. "I had all the time in the world to take him apart with more breaker holds." Daria ruffles Viktoriya's hair and smiles.

12

Cassius is lying on the couch in his rooms when there is a knock on the door and Larina walks in. She strides over to the couch and taps Cassius's legs and sits down next to him. Larina grabs Cassius by the back of the neck and pulls him over so he is leaning on her shoulder, his head resting on the cool leather of her jacket.

"That wasn't fair." Cassius exhales and slumps further onto Larina. "Kaden has no skill in close combat. He's going to get killed if they let him leave like that."

"He still has almost nine years before he can compete." Larina musses Cassius's long hair. "You taught him a more valuable lesson than any other saber style fighter could have."

Cassius smiles and sits back up straight. Just in time to receive a playful arm shot from the former striker. "That fight was wicked though, my little dude. How did you learn to fight a saber?"

"My mom kept developing her style after she stopped fighting." Cassius leans back on the couch and looks up at the ceiling. "The style is called 'Rising Sun' it doesn't combine the three most common fighting styles." Cassius looks over at Larina "It combines all seven styles."

Larina Smiles "I knew there were holes when you sparred." I couldn't understand why you hesitated. Guess I know now, huh?" Cassius's smile widens, then Larina stands up and turns to Cassius "Want to see something cool?" Larina spins away from Cassius, her blonde and fluorescent pink hair spins out behind her and she starts to walk out of the room.

Cassius jumps to his feet and follows Larina out of his rooms. After a few seconds of walking, Larina leads Cassius up a set of back stairs. There is a door at the top, Larina pulls a key out of her jacket pocket and opens the door. The door opens onto the roof of the main house, Cassius can see the entire training yard. Larina walks to the edge of the roof and swings her legs up over the raised ledge that surrounds the entire roof. Cassius walks over to Larina, he leans against the raised edge of the roof and looks down.

"Quite the drop, isn't it?" Larina smiles at the look on Cassius's face. I come up here when I need to clear my head.

Cassius looks up at his striker trainer "Can I ask you a question?"

"You just did." Larina looks down at Cassius, whose scowl sets her chuckling. "Sure, kid, what's on your mind?"

"Do you regret retiring?" the question makes Larina grimace.

"I didn't get a choice, but no, I don't regret it." Larina rubs the back of her left hand. "In my last title fight, I broke my hand. I went from being five feet of pain and fury to being unable to compete in one stroke." Larina shows Cassius her hand, there are three small scars across the back of her wrist. "I had to get bars put into my hand. Which means I couldn't legally compete."

"If you had the option to go back, would you?" Cassius looks out over the training yard.

"No way, I haven't trained properly for two years. I would get myself killed within my first three rounds." Larina laughs, but her laugh dies as she looks down at Cassius. "What's up kid? You're worried about your mom, aren't you?" Cassius nods, making an obvious act of not looking back to Larina. "Your mom won't go back to the ring, she's a brilliant woman. She knows she can't compete anymore."

Cassius nods. "Thanks, I just need a minute. How long do I have before I have to fight again?" he continues to look out over the training fields.

Larina looks at her wrist unit. "You have about ten minutes." She kicks her legs back over the edge and starts to walk towards the door. "I'll come back later to lock up, maybe."

Cassius just stares down into the fields and watches the fighters who had lost their morning bouts train to get better.

Cassius makes his way back to the change rooms outside the ring. Between two of the doors is a holographic screen with the newly condensed ladder. As Cassius looks down the pairings to find his own name, he smiles to see that Vik has made it to the next round. He finds his name paired against Davin, a grappler and striker.

Cassius walks into the change room, Larina must have had his pads brought from his room, he smiles and slips the pads on over his day clothes, not bothering with the black jumpsuit. Cassius walks out to the ring, Davin hasn't come out yet. Cassius climbs the steps and stands next to Daria in the ring. Davin explodes out of his change room and runs to the cage, the young teenager leaps from the floor onto the mat.

Davin stands just over a foot taller than Cassius, and his frame is chiseled and defined from years of training. Daria set the fight and the two boys begin to circle.

"Looks like I got lucky." Davin smiles, showing a mouth guard colored to look like a set sharpened fangs.

"This won't be as fun as you think." Cassius turns to Daria "Hey, why don't I have a mouth guard?"

At that moment, Davin dashes forward and unleashes a spinning back kick at Cassius's head. Spinning under the strike, Cassius drops to his hands and knees turned away from Davin. The larger boy moves to get a cover on Cassius just as he pushes off the ground and drives both of his feet into Davin's stomach. Davin stumbles back a few feet, then he gathers himself for another attack. This time Cassius isn't fast enough, the roundhouse kick connects with his chest and he is thrown across the ring, his back hits the cage and he coughs as he slumps to the ground.

Davin bares his mouth guard and strides towards Cassius, he lifts his right fist and taps his elbow. Thinking Cassius too stunned to be able to counter the move, Davin drops to the mat to deliver a brutal elbow strike to Cassius's face. Cassius manages to get his hands up at the last moment. He pushes Davin's elbow to the side with the back of his right hand, and using the larger boy's momentum he delivers a jarring strike to Davin's right cheekbone. Davin hits the mat and rolls away, trying to make some space, but Cassius isn't having it. Cassius springs up off his back and delivers an express posted slide kick to Davin's ribs.

Cassius grabs Davin's right arm by the wrist and pulls it out of his guard. Holding the other boy's arm out on the mat, Cassius drives his forearm into Davin's elbow. Cassius wraps both of his arms around Davin's injured forearm and torques it backwards, planting his knee in the back of the larger boy's shoulder. Davin grits his teeth and rotates his arm, the additional pressure on the joint causing it to creak and grind. Davin manages to get a grip on Cassius's chest pad and brings his arm down to the mat, slamming Cassius's face off the spring supported canvas. Cassius rolls away as Davin gets to his feet, cradling his damaged arm Davin runs at Cassius. Cassius makes it to his hands and knees before Davin makes contact. Most of the impact from the running knee strike is absorbed by the padding of Cassius's helmet, the rest is absorbed by his nose as something crunches. Cassius lands on his back and Daria steps between the two boys.

Davin tries to sidestep Daria, but two crocked fingers hook into his Trapezius muscle and throw him to the ground. "Stand down, you won." Davin jumps to his feet and tries to push past Daria a second time. "I said stand down!" Daria grabs the boys Trapezius in a pincer grip, then she drives a tiger's-paw into Davin's chest pad followed by a flat palm to his padded helmet. Davin lands hard on his injured shoulder, he cries out and clutches at the decimated joint.

"Feel like pushing it again, kid?" Daria kneels and holds two crooked fingers a hair's breadth above Davin's eyes.

The Cage opens and Nalia hauls Cassius out of the ring and helps him to a seat. She lies his head in Larina's lap and goes to find a cold compress.

Davin's trainer rushes to the ring, but without breaking eye contact with Davin Daria points at the trainer and he freezes.

"I asked you a question. Do you feel like pushing me again? Well?" Daria leans in further, she sets the tips of her viciously sharpened and lacquered nails on Davin's eyeballs. Davin shudders "Careful, kid." Daria whispers.

"No, Master Viper!" Davin shouts. Daria snaps her fingers away from Davin's eyes and pulls him to his feet. She practically throws the boy to his trainer.

"We will talk later." Daria glares at the trainer and stands back up.

Within a few moments Vik comes out of one of the changing rooms. She walks into the ring and looks at Daria "You have a strand of hair floating off your head, front left."

Daria calmly passes her left hand over her head, smoothing the loose strand into place. Viktoriya's opponent is Finn, a disruptor about two years older than Vik. He steps into the ring and bows to Viktoriya, she returns the bow. Devi sets the match and steps back.

Viktoriya studies Finn's form, he is crouched to eliminate the height difference. Disrupter techniques work best on someone your own height. Daria steps into the experimental stance Larina and Nalia are trying to develop to combine striker and breaker motions. Both said their styles suffered, but Vik had seen Cassius use this form in dislocation drills to profound effect. Viktoriya jabs to draw an attack, but she had underestimated the reach advantage of the taller Finn. Finn's arm snaps out and catches Vik around the wrist, his thumbs press into the nerve point in her wrist. Finn pulls Vik towards him and drives his thumb into the inside of her upper arm. His shoulder hits in Vik's armpit and he flips her over his shoulder, Vik lands on her rear end facing away from Finn. The older boy, still holding Vik by the wrist, grinds his thumb in behind Vik's collar bone looking for a submission. Vik kicks her feet but keeps her hand still.

Vik throws her head back and her helmet connects with the inside of Finn's thigh; the impact loosens his grip on the nerve in her collar. She feels Finn lock his grip on her wrist instinctively. Vik uses the locked grip Finn has on her wrist to lift herself into position for an arm bar. Vik pulls herself into the air and kicks her legs out around Finn's arm, she swings her legs across Finn's torso. Her lower leg catches Finn in the chest and throws him further off balance; her upper calf slams into Finn's throat, throwing them to the ground. Vik quickly pushes her lower knee under Finn's elbow and starts to apply pressure. In a real match Vik would have struck the back of her opponents elbow to dislocate the joint.

Finn lifts Vik off the ground and drops her back to the mat. The added force applied to his already strained elbow is too much, the joint gives out with a sickening crunch. Vik releases Finn immediately and the boy rolls away clutching his arm. Vik scrambles to her feet and reassumes her guard. Daria slides across the mat and puts her hand on Finn's shoulder. She looks at his arm, then looks to Vik and nods. Vik drops her guard, then raises her hand over head.

"Oh, yes!" Vik starts to pace with her arms in the air. The cage opens and Devi walks in to collect Vik. Inaudible to anyone but herself murmurs "The Victorian Age has begun."

13

When Devi brings Viktoriya back to where Cassius and their other trainers are gathered. Cassius holds a fist out to Vik, she meets it with one of her own.

"Well, you four have some figuring to do. While I have some recuperating to accomplish. I'll meet you back here for Vik's next match in two hours?" Without waiting for an answer Cassius walks off in the direction of his rooms with an icepack held to his face. Viktoriya lets her trainers walk with her to her rooms. She listens to their recommendations: a hot shower, a light meal, then sleep. Vik closes the door and manages to make it to the couch before collapsing, she drops into the middle of the couch and holds her head in her hands.

That's how Nalia finds the girl two hours later when she comes to check on her. Nalia walks over to the couch and sits on the coffee table across from the girl. She uncomfortably rests her hand on Vik's shoulder.

"Hey Vik, you okay." Nalia looks at Viktoriya, concern written plain on her face. When Vik looks up. Nalia is taken aback by the smile on the young girl's face.

"I liked it." Viktoriya's smile falls from her face and is replaced by a look of horror. "I really hurt Finn, and I liked it."

Nalia smirks, this she can deal with. "Battle fever, happens to some of the best fighters. That can make you a great fighter, but it can also make you stupid. If it hits you in the middle of a fight, your body will function on pure instinct." Vik looks up and locks eyes with Nalia.

"The solution to that, is to train your instincts to the point where they won't get you killed."

"Am I disqualified from the ladder?" Vik starts to pull her padded gloves off her hands, but Nalia stops her.

"You are still in. Get ready for a beatdown derby, girl." Nalia pulls Vik to her feet. "You get to fight Garrick, he's a slider and a striker."

Nalia leads Viktoriya out of her room. Devi, Larina and Cassius are waiting outside. Vik smiles at them and leads the group to the change rooms and the ring.

Garrick is standing in the ring when Vik comes out. She walks up the steps into the cage and bows to the teenager. He smiles and returns the bow.

"I hear you took Finn apart, I didn't know they were teaching you to be a breaker." Garrick straightens back up and offers his wrist to Daria.

Vik scoffs "I could have taken Finn apart before I got here." She offers Daria her wrist. "Last chance to walk away, Garrick."

"No chance." Garrick smirks as Daria sets the fight.

Garrick slides back into a slide style and Vik smiles. Vik rushes Garrick in a grappling stance. Garrick leaps over Vik, his arms swing down and back. Just before Garrick's hands hit the ground behind Vik, she plants both of her hands and snaps her feet up and back. Her heels connect squarely in the middle of Garrick's chest. The impact causes the larger boy to fumble his landing and he lands hard on his neck. Garrick rolls to the side and pops to his feet, he shakes his head and takes up a striker guard. Vik gets to her hands and knees, taking a low grappling guard.

Sitting outside the ring, Cassius smiles and sits forward on his knees. Garrick rushes back in at Vik, he unleashes a spinning axe kick intended to knock Vik's padded helmet into the mat. At the end of his first rotation Garrick sees his mistake, Vik has sidestepped his kick rising out of the low grappling guard and transitioning into a striker form. Her shin connects with his face with a deafening slap. Garrick hits the mat hard and Vik rushes to capitalize. She slides on mat and wraps her left leg around Garrick's, resting her ankle in the back of his knee joint. Vik grabs the strap of Garrick's shin guard and pulls his leg up. She wraps her arms around Garrick's ankle and leans backwards, crushing Garrick's left calf against her ankle and putting immense amounts of pressure on his knee joint.

Daria slides across the mat to check that Garrick can continue the fight, then she taps Vik on the shoulder. Vik lets her head loll back, still maintaining the breaker hold on Garrick's knee. The look in her eyes takes Daria aback, she pushes Vik forward and releases the breaker lock.

Vik stands up and holds her hands over her head. Cassius stands from his chair and cheers. Nalia jumps to her feet as well and runs to the ringside. She unlocks the cage and climbs up. Nalia grabs Vik by the shoulder and leads her out of the ring. The two approach the rest of their group and Vik is beaming.

Nalia takes Viktoriya back to her room. She leaves the girl with instructions to rest and recover her strength. She closes the door softly behind her, but when she turns around Greg Ivanov is striding towards her.

"Her next fight is in three hours. Let her rest." Nalia has to try very hard to sound authoritative when faced with a man as imposing as The Giant.

"I know that, why do you think I'm here?" Greg Ivanov crosses his massive arms and glares at Nalia. "Just let me by."

"Five minutes." Nalia steps aside and The Giant ducks through the doorway.

"Dad!" Viktoriya leaps at her father from behind the door. The Giant spins his daughter off his back and into a bear hug. The little girl calls out with delight and her father carries her to the couch and sits her on his lap.

"Dad, I'm not three anymore." Still giggling, Vik slides off her father's lap and on the small portion of the couch not taken up by the man's enormous frame. "So, final four. Any brilliant advice from the world champion?"

"Just one nugget of wisdom." Greg looks down at his daughter, "Let the beast loose." Greg stands up and starts to walk towards the door.

"What? Are you serious?" Vik jumps to her feet, "You don't even use that in your title matches. This isn't even a real fight!"

Greg turns back to his daughter. "Your opponent is eighteen. He moves on to the pro circuit in three weeks. Your difference in size and skill make it a fight to fatality. At least for you." He smiles "besides, your ref is the Viper, she will have no problem putting you down if she has to."

"Yes, sir." Vik steps onto the coffee table, then drops into a crossed leg meditative pose. Greg looks away as she closes her eyes.

The Giant walks back through the door and looks down at Nalia, "Now don't let anyone into that room. Viktoriya is meditating and I fear for the life of anyone who goes in there until after this match." He starts to walk away from Nalia when he pauses, he spins back around and points at the door, "You would do well to disregard anything you hear as well." With that, Greg walks to a set of stairs and ascends to the upper floor.

"What was that all about?" Nalia mutters as she drops to the ground and pulls a notebook from a pocket. She starts to jot notes on her observations of Cassius and Vik's fights, trying to find ways of making the move transitions flawless. The three trainers had already come up with hybrid guards for all the style combinations, however Nalia was sure they were missing something. Nalia knows that there is something Cassius has holding back, but she can't figure out what that something may be. Nalia passes the next three hours trying to apply her knowledge of slide style's fluid, dancelike motions to smooth these weaknesses. She finds that some of the gaps can be filled, but still others remain weak points in the style.

Inside the room, all is still. Inside Viktoriya, however there is no peace. Viktoriya uses the techniques her father had taught her to visualize a place of absolute nothingness, an endless void inside her mind. Into this place of total absence, Viktoriya conjures a twenty-five-sided steel cage. The number of sides was important for some reason, Vik was too concerned with making sure there were exactly twenty-five side to contemplate if she even knew why.

When the floating steel cage has been formed, darkness from the surrounding void appears to flow in between the chain links. The liquid darkness flows across the floor of the cage, pooling in the center of the cage floor. The darkness coagulates into a humanoid shape with long spindly limbs and an emaciated torso. Stringy black hair hangs over a gaunt, hard boned face. The thing's large head snaps up and locks eyes with Viktoriya, the creature starts to change as it crawls towards Vik. The creature's hair turns a brilliant gold and begins to curl, it's emaciated form fills out to that of a healthily curvy woman. By the time the creature reaches the near side of the cage it resembles a beautiful woman in her late teens.

"Kalman" Vik sneers at the woman inside the cage.

"Come to stare again, little girl?" the strange creature spins in a slow circle.

"No, I'm here to use you." Vik takes another step towards the cage and the creature slams itself against the chain link.

"You think you can use me? I am you!" the creature bares its jagged razor-sharp teeth.

"You are just a part of me, creature and you will submit." Viktoriya kicks the creature in the chest as she steps into the cage, she passes through the chain link as if she is made of smoke.

The creature in the cage has lost its glamour. It leaps at her, sharp claws and teeth flashing. Vik grabs the creature by its wrist, she wrenches the creature forward and drives her fist into its throat. The monster collapses and Vik mounts it. Planting her knees on the creature's elbows, Vik unleashes a flurry of blows to its face. The creature gurgles and Viktoriya turns it over. Vik kneels on both the creature's elbows and interlocks her hands in front of its face, she leans backwards and the creature screams.

"I submit!" it screams and gnashes her teeth. The creature's body pools into black liquid and is absorbed by Viktoriya's skin. Vik's back arches and she screams. In her head, the creatures voice echoes "For now…"

Vik's eyes snap open. She vaults off the coffee table and walks to the door. She strides through the door and walks to towards the change rooms. Nalia calls after her.

"Hey, your match isn't for another fifteen minutes, where are you going?" Nalia jumps to her feet then Vik turns to look at her. Nalia freezes when she sees the murderous fury in Vik's eyes. Vik turns back around and stalks off down the hall.

Vik kicks through the door to a change room, she starts to pull her pads off and moves towards the shower. After scrubbing with near boiling water, Vik finds a panel connected to a pair of speakers. In a few moments, the sounds of heavy drums and a harsh violin fill the air. Viktoriya searches the cabinets until she finds a palette of body paints. Using a heavy black paint Vik paints her face, arms, and legs. Vik highlights her knuckles, knees, and elbows with white paint. Using a vibrant red paint Vik draws two large eyes around her own, and a freakish smile that travels from one ear to the other. Vik walks to the door at the end of the hall but it doesn't open. She crosses her legs and sits in front of the door until it hisses open.

Viktoriya comes out of her door on all fours, she crawls up the steps and summersaults into the middle of the ring. Vik pops up into a crouch across from Blaine, her opponent is severely taken aback by her appearance. Blaine is wearing no pads. The only remnant of the heavy padding are the gloves on his hands, designed more to soften strikes than to protect the hands. Vik is also only wearing her padded gloves.

Daria looks down to reprimand Vik, but a motion out of the corner of her eye stops her. Greg is standing between the ring and the chairs where the other onlookers are sitting. He simply shakes his head and Daria straightens up and sets the match. The two opponents rush each other at full tilt.

Blaine closes in on Vik in two strides, he lashes out with a spinning high kick, Vik drops to her knees and slides under Blaine's leg. Vik lashes out with a debilitating knuckle strike to the inside of his other thigh, Blaine drops to the ground. Instead of capitalizing, Viktoriya jumps to her feet and stalks Blaine jeering at him and motioning for him to get up. When Blaine tries to rise, Vik kicks him in the side of the head. He drops back to the mat and Daria moves to check on him.

Vik grabs Blaine's ankle and wrenches it to the side, straining the tendons and damages the joint. Blaine snaps his other foot up and catches Viktoriya under the jaw, throwing her off him. Vik uses the momentum of the strike to roll to the edge of the ring as Blaine rolls onto his back. When he tries to stand the muscle cramp in his thigh and damaged ankle cause him to fall back down to the mat. Vik bares her teeth and runs across the ring, she throws herself into the air over Blaine. Blaine raises his knees, expecting Vik to attempt to strike his torso. Vik plants her hand on Blaine's knees and vaults over the downed boy, the look of shock on his face makes Vik burst into hysterical laughter. When she lands on the mat past Blaine Vik kicks off the cage wall and spins back around, she drops a vicious axe kick towards Blaine's face. Blaine barely manages to get his hands up over his face to soften the blow. He pushes Vik's foot up and away trying to create some pace, but that opens his head to a knee drop. Vik slams her knee into Blaine brow, splitting the skin above his left eye. Vik stands back up and starts to pace the inside of the ring, Blaine rolls on the floor holding his face.

Daria steps between Vik and her prey, she bares her teeth and snarls. Daria holds a hand out towards Vik, warding her off. Daria signals to have the cage opened. Two trainers rush forward and open the cage, they pull Blaine out of the cage and help him limp away from the ring. Daria steps back from Vik and looks around for Greg. She spots him walking up to the cage behind Viktoriya. Greg slams his hands on the cage and Vik spins around, at that moment Daria slides out of the cage and the opening is locked once again.

Daria walks over to Greg and whispers in his ear "What the hell is that?" she points back to where Vik is sitting in the center of the ring, legs crossed and head lolling back.

"That is her Beast." Greg whispers back as he leads Daria away from the ring. "My grandfather was the first Ivanov to encounter The Beast. It is a part of us, a deep well of rage, strength, and instinct.

As a child, I was taught to keep The Beast contained inside me. I started to teach Vik when she was four years old. Through meditation, we are able to harness it for additional power. However, just like battle fever we revert to basic animalistic instinct. The Beast is unpredictable, which is why I haven't used it in years. It can smooth out a steep learning curve, but you can't paint with a sledgehammer."

"So, Vik has harnessed this 'Beast'? how long will she be like this?" Daria looks back at Viktoriya, who is now prowling the edges of the cage on all fours.

"She will be like that for a couple hours." Greg crosses his arms "I would suggest starting the next fight. Vik's Beast is hungry."

Daria turns back to the ring and sees Vik lying spread-eagled on the mat.

"Fine, but I need a better answer than that if I'm going to keep training her." Daria walks away from The Giant and shouts for one of the trainers. A few terse words send the trainer running for Vik's next opponent.

14

Mike walks through the door and up towards the ring, lost in thought trying to plan for a fight against a tank like Blaine. When he steps into the ring and sees Vik sitting on the floor in body paint he freezes. Daria motions to him and he climbs the last step and walks into the ring.

Daria leans in and whispers "Don't completely embarrass yourself, ok?" Daria takes his wrist and the Cage closes. Daria set the match and Vik explodes off the mat.

Her initial lunge allows Mike to execute a throw and flip the small girl over his shoulder. He moves to drop a knee on her face, but Vik manages to snap her feet up and catches Mike in the side of the head. He falls over and rolls away from Vik, who jackknifes to her feet and stalks across the ring to circle Mike. When Mike starts to rise Viktoriya kicks at his head. Mike sees the kick coming and he catches her leg. Driving his thumb into the back of Vik's leg, Mike forces Vik to turn her back. Mike launches himself at Vik, aiming a strike to the base of her skull. Vik drops to the ground before the strike lands, she plants her hands and strikes Mike in the chest with her feet. The man's momentum coupled with Vik's kick sends him slamming into the cage wall. He catches himself, but Viktoriya jumps on him and drives her knees into his back.

Mike reaches over his shoulder and grabs Vik by the hair. He jumps back from the cage and lands on Vik. She coughs as he rolls off her and away. Mike straddles Vik and rains punches down on her guard. Vik takes a strike to the jaw, but she manages to land a strike on

Mike's small ribs. Mike grunts, but he keeps up his assault. Within seconds Vik's teeth are red with blood. Daria slides in to check on Vik, Mike's momentary hesitation is all Vik needs. Vik drives her knee into Mike's groin, then strikes at him with both hands. Mike's head rocks back and Vik strikes again with both her fists, this time to his stomach. Vik hauls herself off the mat and headbutts Mike. Vik slides out from under Mike and kicks him in the side of the head. Mike rolls away and stays in a low guard, Vik turns to face him. The two circle one another for a few seconds, then Vik lunges in. Mike grabs Vik by the throat and slams her onto the mat, he pulls the small girl back up and slams her again. This time Vik lies on the mat, dazed. Daria slides in and ends the fight, Mike staggers to the edge of the ring and down the stairs.

"What is that thing?" Mike asks his trainer when he comes to help him down the stairs. His trainer doesn't say anything as he swiftly guides the young man out of the room.

Daria dashes to the opening of the cage and locks it behind herself. She jumps off the stairs and strides over to Greg. "Can I leave her in the ring without worrying she'll escape and kill someone?"

"Viktoriya and her Beast will be perfectly safe in there." Greg looks at his daughter and sighs. "I suppose I owe you some explanations, no?"

"You certainly do, meet me in my office. I have to deal with her trainers." Daria turns away and jogs to intercept the group heading towards the ring. "I wouldn't do that if I were you."

"What do you mean?" Devi stops. The rest of the group freezes in place as well.

"Do not open that cage." Daria points back towards Vik. "She isn't herself, she needs some time to cool down. I'll look after her."

"Yes, Master Viper." Nalia nods to her companions and they walk away.

Daria turns to look at Vik, just now sitting up in the ring. She watches Vik prowl the ring for a few seconds, then Daria turns to leave. She leaves the lights in the room on.

Nalia, Devi, Larina, and Cassius have gathered in the dining hall, each has a half-eaten sandwich sitting in front of them. Nalia takes a sip of her water and fills the rest of the group in on her theory.

"There are stories of fighters in the old world who would channel the spirits of heroes or demons. They were able to use that power in important fights to give themselves more strength and stamina. I think that is what we saw today. Her father is a world champion, we should have expected her to have something up her sleeve."

Cassius takes a sip from his cup and clears his throat, "So you think she will be okay then?"

"Who's going to be okay?" Vik walks up and takes her seat on the bench, everyone stares at her as she steals the remainder of Cassius's sandwich and shoves it into her mouth.

"So, are you still crazy, or are you better?" Cassius scowls at Vik when she picks up his mug and drinks from it.

"I'm fine. You won't be seeing that side of me for a while, I promise." Vik reaches across the table to steal Larina's sandwich, but the older woman raps her knuckles.

"Not a sufficient answer." Larina growls and Vik's eyes widen.

"Okay, fine." Vik explains about The Beast, the hereditary affliction that causes what her friends had seen. Avoiding specifics when possible. The group sits in silence absorbing the tale with great interest.

The next day, Greg leaves the academy, as his car pulls up in the drive he turns to Daria. "Take care of my daughter. She will learn well under you."

Daria smiles and playfully punches The Giant in the shoulder. "Come back some time, I know she loves seeing you."

Greg smiles and climbs down into the back seat of his customized car; the front passenger's seat has been removed to make additional room for his massive frame.

"I mean it, come back soon." Daria waves as the car pulls away from the main house. She turns and walks back to the doors; just inside Elizabeth is waiting. A sheaf of paper clutched in one hand.

"Daria, I need you to sign these. Then we have a fighter who is finishing his training. We need you to supervise his graduation and help him set up his first fight." El hands the papers over to Daria, who starts to flip through them as she walks toward the training yard.

"We have a lot more work to do than I thought, huh?" Daria pushes through the doors to the yard and nods to a pair of fighters, they square off and begin to spar on the grass. Daria quickly signs the papers and hands them back to Elizabeth. "A whole lot more work."

15

Cassius's hair whips out as Viktoriya's fist crashes across his cheek bone, he drops to the mat as Vik twists the grapple to flip on top of him. She strikes down at Cassius, but he grabs her arm and kicks her up over him. Her back hits the mat and she immediately kips up, spinning to kick Cassius in the face. Cassius has rolled out of the way and as he stands, he pulls his hand through his hair. The tail ends just past the length of his arm. Cassius starts to run at the cage walls, his momentum carries him up onto the side of the cage and he jumps off and kicks out towards Vik's chest.

Viktoriya leans back and Cassius's kick flies over her head, she drops to her knees and Cassius flies completely over her. Vik reaches up and grabs Cassius's hair, she pulls and he topples to the mat. Vik capitalizes instantly, vaulting on top of Cassius, and raining strikes down on his guard. Larina slams on the mat to call the fight.

"Well done Vik! Great use of your height difference. Cassius, get your bloody hair cut!" Larina walks up behind Cassius and yanks his hair.

"Yeah. It's grown longer again, huh?" Cassius reaches behind his head and starts to braid his dark brown hair. "It's shorter once it's braided." Cassius pulls his braid out and it ends a little past his elbow.

"You're just getting lazy and hope El won't notice. Do you not remember what she did last time you did that?" Vik yanks Cassius's braid and he grits his teeth.

"Yeah, she made me run laps with weight straps." Cassius shudders.

"That's a great suggestion." El steps out from behind Devirian and Cassius smiles timidly

"Hey, El…" Cassius unconsciously twists the brass ring holding his hair in place.

El pulls a pair of scissors out of her pocket and spins them on her finger "It's been over two months since I cut that hazard for you."

Cassius pulls his braid over his shoulder, the thick rope of hair ends just above his abdominal muscles, "I left the end unbraided."

"Don't forget again." El turns to Cassius, "Snip, snip, Rapunzel." She steps up and grabs Cassius's braid, the scissors flash and four inches of dark brown hair fall to the ground.

In the eleven years Cassius and Vik had been training under Larina, Devirian, and Nalia he had grown into a man. Looking over at Viktoriya, Cassius can not help but linger on the evidence of her maturity. Vik notices his gaze and catches his eye, she smiles and punches him in the arm.

Devi and Larina exchange a knowing look and Devirian smirks. Larina makes a choking noise, then covers it up by clearing her throat. "Cassius, it's your birthday today, isn't it?"

Cassius looks up, trying to remember what day it is. "Yeah, I guess it is, huh?"

"That means you are eighteen, old enough to test out." El smiles and flicks on her wrist unit. "It's been a long road, and I know it hasn't been easy." El turns to the group of trainers, "Just let me know when you think he's ready and I'll set up the test."

Nalia steps forward, "He'll be ready to test tomorrow." Everyone looks at her, aghast. "You all know as well as I do that Cass was ready months ago. The waiting was just a formality." Nalia turns to her two fighters and smiles. In fact, both of them are ready to test out."

"Sounds good, I'll let Master Viper know and set the testing for tomorrow after morning meal." El taps keys on her wrist unit. She no longer needs to go back to a desk unit to perform most of her duties, which enables her to be out among her trainers. Which is good, because under Master Viper the academy has exploded in population. The mostly empty fighter's dorms are now bustling at all hours of the day and night with the comings and goings of over seventy young fighters and their trainers.

Nalia turns to her fighters, "In honour of both Cass's birthday, and your imminent testing. You can both take the rest of the day off."

Cassius beams and bows to Nalia. "Thank you, Master Nalia."

Larina steps forward with a small black box in one hand "This is for you." She puts the small box in Cassius's hand, she has to look up at him now, so she yanks his braid to bring him down to whisper in his ear. "This is still the only one, I want it back before you leave." Larina lets go of Cassius's hair and turns to Viktoriya. "Go get something to eat and get some rest." Her omnipresent smirk widens into a grin.

Vik bows to Larina as Cassius opens the small box she had given him, cradling it in his hand to conceal the contents. Inside the box is a small brass key on a silver chain. Cassius bows low to Larina and she laughs.

"Get out of here, hit the showers." Devi waves his hand dismissively.

"Race you." Viktoriya smirks and takes off in an explosive sprint.

"Hey!" Cassius Runs after Vik, his long legs carrying him across the training ground at an impressive pace.

Vik makes it back to the main house just before Cassius, kicking off the stone wall next to the showers she spins around and lands in time to watch Cassius jog the last few paces to her.

"That was cheap." Cassius leans back and takes a deep breath.

"It's called winning. I swear your sense of 'honour' is going to get you killed." Vik taps out some light combo work against Cassius's torso.

"This isn't a ring match." Cassius starts to lightly deflect Vik's strikes. "Meet me outside our rooms in five minutes?"

"If we are done for the day it will take me a bit more than five." Vik turns and walks towards the women's showers.

"I wouldn't say we are totally done for today." Cassius calls after her.

"I'm still taking longer than five minutes." Vik gives Cassius a one finger salute as she walks away. Cassius laughs and turns to go have a shower.

Five minutes later, Cassius is leaning in his door frame waiting. Exactly five minutes later, Vik opens her door and smiles at Cassius. "Oh, have you been waiting long?"

"No, I just got here myself actually." Cassius and Vik stare each other down until they burst into simultaneous laughter.

"You have something to show me?" Vik smirks as Cassius cantilevers himself off the door frame and waves for her to follow him. He leads her down a winding hallway and her heartrate kicks up a touch. Cassius climbs a set of steps and opens a door Vik has never seen.

Vik steps out onto the roof and the warm June wind ruffles her hair. The sun is just starting to fall from the sky and the expansive blue sets Vik's head spinning. Cassius closes the door behind her and locks it again.

"I came up here during the first ladder." Cassius looks out over the edge of the roof, "That was when I decided I was going to be a world champion. That I would go after what I wanted, and not just wait for it to come to me."

Vik smirks. "Well you sure took your sweet time with this." Vik walks up to stand beside Cassius at the raised edge of the roof.

"Took my time with what?" Cassius turns to look at Viktoriya. Vik is already looking at him, he freezes when they lock eyes. Viktoriya sighs, and she kisses him full on the lips.

Vik feels Cassius freeze up. Was he not expecting this? Then Cassius comes to life, one of his long arms wraps around her waist pulling her closer to him. Vik reaches up behind Cassius and twists the brass band keeping his hair in check. Cassius's hair untwines as the ring falls to the soft sand of the rooftop. Vik twines her fingers in Cassius's dark brown mane and holds him to her. After a few seconds the pair break apart, Vik smiles as Cassius blushes and tucks his hair back behind his ears

"Sorry if I ruined your delivery." Vik blows a lock of navy-blue hair out of her eyes.

"To be honest, that was better than anything I could have come up with." Cassius tucks his hair behind his ears, but there is no hair to tuck. This repeated action makes Vik giggle.

"Want to do it again?" Vik steps forward and rests her hand on Cassius's cheek. Cassius kisses her and they hold one another close as the sun sets behind then.

16

Then next morning, Cassius and Vik have to jog through the halls to make it to breakfast on time. When they arrive Larina has a conspiratorial grin plastered on her petite face.

"We were out doing warm ups." Vik slides onto her seat on the bench and starts shoveling boiled eggs into her mouth one whole egg at a time. A vast improvement in Nalia's eyes, over the two eggs she would cram in at a time even a month previous.

"Where's your hair ring, pretty boy?" Larina's grin isn't going anywhere anytime soon.

Cassius's eyes widen as the image of his hair ring sitting in the sand on the roof flashes through his mind. He recovers quickly and runs his hand through his thick mane. "It's in my room, I wanted to get a breeze going while I was running."

"Well your testing is right after this so I advise, against my better judgment mind you, that you pick up the pace on that plate." Nalia grimaces as Cassius smiles and begins to inhale the food on his tray. In a few minutes, he picks up the last piece of his meal, a bright green apple, and rushes from the dining hall.

Larina turns on Viktoriya next. "Warm ups, huh?"

"Yep. Warm ups" Vik says in between mouthfuls of crisp potato cubes.

Two minutes later, Cassius dashes back into the room and jumps into his seat at the bench. "Got it." Cassius holds the ring up to show his trainers, and Vik snatches it from his hand. "Hey!" Cassius grabs for his hair ring, but Vik pulls it away and flicks a pressure point in his wrist. She sticks her tongue out at him while he tries to shake feeling back into his hand.

"Alright you two, lets get going." Nalia stands up and walks out of the room, the rest of the group follows her out into the yard.

Daria and El are standing in the yard. Flanking the two women are a man and a woman, the man looks a year or two older than Cassius. The woman is about Viktoriya's age, but she is about a foot shorter than Vik. Daria steps forward and bows to Cassius, and then Vik.

"Congratulations, and welcome to your last challenge at this academy." Daria motions to the man and he steps forward. "This is Apollo, regional champion from New Paris." She signals to the woman beside El and she steps forward. "This is Bianca, regional women's champion from North Berlin."

El steps forward she walks in a circle, stabbing plastic stakes into the grass. "If you aren't good enough to be regional champions at least, you aren't ready to test out." El comes back to stand beside Daria, "First to tap or ring out looses. Cassius, you're up."

Cassius turns to Vik, "I need my hair ring back." He holds his hand out, but Viktoriya moves around behind him and gathers his hair. She opens the ring and slides it up to the nape of Cassius's neck. Vik twists the sides of the ring until it cinches tight on Cassius's hair. He smiles at her and steps into the circle. Cassius bows to Apollo, who bows in response. The two men offer their hands to Daria and she sets the match.

Cassius rushes Apollo before the other man can assume any proper guard. Apollo snaps a straight jab out at Cassius's face, but he drops under the strike. Cassius spins as he drops under Apollo's arm, he plants his hands and kicks up and back. Both of his feet catch Apollo in the chest, the strike sends Apollo into the air as Cassius spins back around. Apollo manages to land on his feet inside the circle, but he isn't ready when Cassius charges again. Apollo throws out a cross with his left arm, Cassius sidesteps the strike and gets his arm up under Apollo's guard. Cassius's hand wraps around Apollo's throat and constricts. As Apollo reaches for his throat, Cassius uses his massive leg muscles to propel both men into the air. When Cassius comes back down, he slams Apollo shoulders first into the ground outside the circle, then lands on him with one knee. Apollo coughs and flecks of crimson blood spray into the air.

Daria blows on a whistle and Cassius lifts himself off Apollo; he offers the defeated man his hand. Apollo takes Cassius's hand and struggles to his feet. Cassius bows and Apollo returns the curtesy. Bianca steps into the circle as Cassius leaves. Cassius holds his hand up and Vik claps it. Then he drops his hand, their hands meet again at the bottom of the swing in another clap.

Vik and Bianca bow to each other and Daria steps in to set the fight. Viktoriya rushes in with a copy of Cassius's attack. Bianca, anticipating the same strategy, fires off a low kick. However, Vik jumps and plants a side kick in between Bianca's eyes. The woman drops to the grass and Vik grabs her by the ankles.

Cassius's eyes widen as he sees what Vik is trying to do. "Giants hammer." Cassius murmurs.

Devirian's eyes widen and his jaw drops open. "No way!"

Vik starts to spin, dragging Bianca across the grass and gaining speed. After two rotations, Bianca is off the ground, then she comes to. Bianca quickly grasps her situation and she cries out in terror. Vik grits her teeth and stares at Bianca.

"Do you yield, or do I let you fly?" Vik loosens her grip on Bianca's left ankle.

"I yield!" Bianca shouts and Daria blows her whistle. Vik slows down until Bianca's shoulders scrub on the grass, then she lets go and Bianca rolls away across the grass. Bianca jumps to her feet and bows to Vik. Vik bows to Bianca, then raises her arms over head and paces in the circle.

"Well done, both of you." El steps towards the ring, clapping. She pulls two large envelopes from under her arm and passes one to Apollo, and one to Bianca. The two fighters nod and turn towards the main house.

Daria steps next to El and motions to Cassius, "Come with me kind, Vik you go with El. We need to speak about your future."

Cassius looks at Vik. After training with her for years, there isn't much she can get past him. Cassius gives Vik a hug, then turns to follow Daria back into the main house. El smiles at Viktoriya and gestures for her to follow. El takes Vik to her office, the space shows the signs of the times. The once spotless space is now littered with piles of paper and memory chips. Vik takes a seat at the near side of the desk and waits for El to sit. When El drops into her chair, the added weight of her growing responsibilities is far more visible.

"So, at this point you have some options." El pulls out a stack of papers and divides them into three separate piles. She taps one of the stacks. "This is a contract that offers you the option to stay here and train fighters. This next is a contract that offers financial assistance to get into a regional championship, with eighty percent of that assistance being repaid by you within the first year. And this final contract provides the same financial support as the last contract, except you are not expected to repay that assistance."

Vik leans over. "What's the catch?"

El laughs, "The catch is that you have to get a tattoo. A specific marking to show where you trained."

Vik tilts her head to the side and is silent for a moment. "I do have one question." Vik lifts her head to look at El "Does anyone ever pick the middle contract?"

El laughs again, "Not many, but some people are weird about their skin."

"Where do I sign?" Vik pulls the third contract towards herself and looks around for a pen.

"Last page." El passes a pen case to her, there is a thumbprint scanner on the case, as well as on the pen itself. Vik holds the pen case over a document identification code, the case clicks and a light comes on under the thumbprint scanner on the case. When Vik presses her thumb to the top of the case, it slides open. Vik pulls out the pen and aligns her hand so her thumb is on the reader in the pen, the tip clicks out and Vik signs her name. She puts the pen back in the box and it slides shut and beeps. Vik takes the pen case and slides it into a slot on a small safe, then scans her thumb. The safe clicks open and El removes several tattoo patches. They all contain the same image, a stylized snake's head with dripping fangs. Vik looks at the tattoo design, then contemplates sizing, she picks a five-inch square patch and nods her head. El packs the rest of the patches back into the safe. She closes the safe and turns back to Viktoriya. "Do you know where you want to put it?"

"It has to be visible when I fight, right? But not all the time?" Vik looks up at El.

"That is true." El nods. Vik stands up and pulls her shirt off. El's mouth drops open.

"Can you help me get it on straight? It would be lame to have a crooked tattoo." Vik holds the tattoo patch out to El, who takes it and nods. "Thank you." Vik turns around and points over her shoulder. "Could you put it just above my bra? I won't be wearing anything much bigger when I fight in a ring."

"Sure." El steps up and peels the backing of the tattoo patch, "What about when you do that thing? What do you call it again?" El lines the patch up perfectly with Vik's spine and sticks it down.

"The Beast, Kalman. When I do the paint, I'll make sure it's there, probably go over it with white or something." Vik looks over her shoulder, "Ready?"

"Yeah, here we go." El presses a button and a high intensity laser races across the patch, and by the time Vik flinches the patch is finished. Vik cries out in pain and El tears away the patch. The laser activated ink has burrowed into Vik's skin, and while the area around the tattoo is reddening, the tattoo is clean and will heal quickly.

Vik hugs El, then throws her shirt back on and rushes from the room. In the hall between their old rooms, Cassius is waiting when Vik turns the corner. Vik smiles at him. As she approaches Cassius he lifts his left hand, the snake's head tattoo is deep black on his reddened hand. Vik steps up to him and grabs him by the front of his shirt.

"Let me show you mine." Vik smiles like a fool and pushes through the door into Cassius's rooms.

17

The next morning, Cassius wakes and packs his belongings in the same scruffy backpack he brought with him eleven years ago. He takes one last look at the rooms that had been his home for over half his life. He pulls open the door and practically runs into Larina.

"Master Larina?" Cassius looks down at the short woman.

"Ah, Cassius." Larina looks up at him and smiles "Where's my key?" Cassius pulls the key out of his shirt and pulls the chain over his head. He hands the key to Larina and she smiles. "Oh, and Vik's looking for you." Larina smirks and turns to walk down the hall.

"Master Larina!" Cassius calls after her and she freezes. "I'm going to miss you, and thank you for everything you've done for me."

"Damn it kid. Why did you have to go and say that?" Larina wipes her face on her leather jacket, she takes a laboured breath and waves as she starts walking again. "I'll miss you too, kid. Now get moving, don't leave a woman waiting."

Cassius smiles and heads towards the main hall. When Cassius emerges from under the stairs, Viktoriya spins around in the middle of the room. Her smile lights up the room.

As Cassius walks up to her, Daria's office doors open above them. She leans over the railing and waves "Cassius. Glad I caught you before you left. Can I have a word with you?" Cassius smiles at Vik and jogs up the steps.

"What can I do for you Master Viper?" Cassius leans on the railing and looks at Daria, silver has started to spread through her once blood red hair. Daria sighs and looks down at Viktoriya.

"You know, I've known that girl since she was a babe in arms." Daria runs a hand through her hair and leans on the rail. "I just signed paperwork that will let her get herself killed."

"Vik is stronger than a lot of the fighters who have walked through those doors. She's going to be fine." Cassius looks down at Vik, she's absorbed by something on her wrist unit.

"I need you to promise me something." Daria looks back up at Cassius, her gaze makes him stand up straight.

"I won't be able to keep her from fighting, she wants this more than I do." Cassius rubs at his tattoo, the skin around it is still red, but it is healing quickly.

"Just look out for her, okay?" Daria pounds her fist on the railing, the crunch of bone makes her wince. "Damn it to hell." Daria looks at her hand, the telltale purple of fractured bone is already spreading. Daria shoves her hand in her pocket and looks back up to Cassius. "So, what's your first move when you get out of here?"

Cassius relaxes and leans back on the rail. "Until yesterday, I was planning to just go to the nearest arena and sign up for the regionals. But now, I honestly don't know."

"Does that hickey have something to do with your change of heart?" Daria smiles at Cassius as he reaches for the side of his neck. "Before you ask, it's not that bad, I just have an eye for it."

Cassius lets his hand drop from his neck. "It does have something to do with it, yes. But we haven't really talked about that yet. I was just about to when you called me."

"Best get back to it then." Daria flick open her wrist unit and taps a few keys, "Her ride will be delayed a few moments. Better make it count."

"Yes, master Viper." Cassius starts to turn away, then he smirks and looks back. "It would be a shame if El found out about your hand from anyone other than you…"

"Get moving, I can still kick your ass with one hand." Daria smiles as Cassius jogs back down the stairs.

When he reaches the bottom step, Cassius jumps. He lands with a shoulder roll and pops to his feet in front of Vik. She looks up from her wrist unit and smiles. "Hey." Vik nods up at the railing, "What was all that about?"

Cassius smirks, "She wanted me to give you a hard time about the hickey you left on my neck." Vik's hands go to her mouth and she gasps. Cassius laughs, then he lowers his voice. "But in all honesty, she just asked the question I have been wracking my brain over since you left yesterday. 'Now What?'"

"What do you mean?" Vik tilts her head and looks at Cassius in confusion.

"Well, until yesterday I had resigned myself to never seeing you again. Then yesterday happened. What are you planning to do when you walk out those doors?"

"I am going to New Yuma. The regionals there start in two weeks, so I still have time to register." Vik squeezes Cassius's hands, "Will you come with me to New Yuma?"

Cassius smiles "It would be my pleasure to go to New Yuma with you." Vik smiles and Cassius kisses her.

"Looks like you two are buying drinks tonight!" Larina is walking towards Cassius and Vik, but her back is turned and she is pointing at Nalia and Devi. Nalia is smirking, one eyebrow raised as she looks at the two fighters. Vik and Cassius quickly step apart, but Larina steps up to them and wraps her arms over their shoulders. Larina looks from Vik to Cassius, then back at Vik. "I told these two you would be an item when you walked out of here today. They didn't believe me, so now they are buying me drinks!"

"So, where is our dynamic duo headed? Devirian interlaces his fingers behind his head.

Vik smiles at her trainers "We are going to New Yuma to register for regionals."

Nalia whistles, "New Yuma huh? Sounds like fun."

Cassius looks over at Vik "If you guys want to come out for the night you are welcome."

"Hell yeah!" Larina Throws her arms in the air, "Party!" She throws her arms around Vik and Cassius "Let's go already!"

As the group walks out the front doors, a long black limo glides into the driveway on fifteen-inch, chrome rims. Vik's father's driver steps out of the cab of the limo and opens the trunk and the back door. When Vik walks up with her bags, the driver hands her a memory chip and whispers in her ear. "A message from Master Giant, of a personal nature as I understand." Vik nods to the driver.

"Thank you, Felix. How is my father?" Vik puts her bags in the trunk of the car.

"He is doing well mistress, he left for Rome night before last. He expressed his regrets at not being able to come in person today, hence the message I would suppose." Felix helps Vik into the limo and turns to greet the rest of the Group. Viktoriya slides into the seat nearest the far door and, more importantly, the window. Vik immediately rolls the window down and lets a light breeze into the darkened interior.

"Good to see you again, Felix." Cassius steps forward and shakes the old driver's hand.

"You as well, Master Slade." Felix holds his hand out for Cassius's pack. Cassius hands the bag to the old man and climbs down into the limo next to Viktoriya.

Larina, Devirian, and Nalia all pile in next, they sit along the side of the limo on a long bench seat. Felix closes the limos door and trunk, then he walks to the front of the vehicle and starts to pull out of the driveway. Cassius and Vik look back at the Academy, bidding the familiar place farewell.

The drive from the academy to New Yuma takes about four hours, during which time Larina changes the music selection eight times, stands up through the sun roof twice, and eats what Cassius can only assume is her own body weight in fresh pastries. Nalia and Vik spend most of the trip on their wrist units. Devi falls asleep half an hour out from the academy, he snores quietly in the corner, dead to the world. Cassius spends an hour on his wrist unit, considering accommodations in New Yuma. After serving himself a strong coffee from the on-board bar, Cassius stares out the windows at nothing, nursing his coffee until it goes cold in the mug.

18

When the limo pulls into New Yuma, all the occupants save Felix have fallen asleep. Felix pulls the vehicle up in front of a high-end hotel, climbing out of the cab he stretches. These long drives are starting to take a toll on his weary frame. He waves to a young porter and the boy runs over to him.

"How may I help you sir?" the porter's vest is a deep violet with golden buttons. Felix feels sorry for the boy. The get up makes him look young, and foolish.

"I need to secure three rooms for tonight, and one for a few more nights." Felix outlines the requirements for the rooms and the boy nods every so often. Finally, Felix hands the boy a credit card. The boy turns to run and make the arrangements, and Felix calls him back.

"Yes sir?" the porter looks concerned.

"If you can remember that whole thing and get it right after the fight with the desk staff, I have a better job for you." Felix smiles at the boy and the porter nods and dashes into the hotel. A few moments later, a severe looking man slightly younger than Felix strides out of the front of the hotel. The young porter is hot on the older man's trail, they stop in front of Felix and the man in the suit splutters.

"Who are you, to just pull in here and expect us to have rooms open on such short notice? This is a high-end establishment, you know." The man in the suit offers Felix the card he had given to the porter.

Felix slowly clears his throat "I know exactly the calibre of establishment this is. My name is Felix, I am the personal driver of the world champion, Greg 'The Giant' Ivanov."

The man in the suit pales, "I'm very sorry sir, I was unaware." Before the man can retract his hand, Felix takes his card back and nods towards the porter.

"What was my request? To the letter, if you please." Felix listens intently as the boy recites every one of Felix's requests, not even the most outlandish request was left out. "How about that job, kid? Violet isn't your color."

The porter beams and unbuttons his vest and hands it to the man in the suit. "Consider this my resignation." The boy steps over to Felix and shakes the old man's hand.

Felix sends the boy to the passenger's side of the cab and smiles at the man in the suit. "Don't expect our patronage or recommendation in the future." Felix bows to the other man and climbs back into the cab of the limo. He looks at the boy sitting in the passenger's seat. "How do you feel about learning to be a driver?"

"Anything will be better than working there." The boy points his thumb over his shoulder as they pull away from the hotel. "What you did back there was amazing."

"First lesson, any power we have comes from who we work for. I work for Master Ivanov, so I enjoy some liberties. You, on the other hand, work for me which provides you exactly zero power." Felix looks over at the boy. The fool is grinning ear to ear. "Your first task is to memorize the map of every major city. From there you will move on to learning how to navigate tin town streets. Then I'll teach you how to drive the car. You have most of the etiquette training you will need, however so you have an advantage." Felix continues to lecture the boy, then a thought occurs to him. "What's your name, kid?"

"My name is Bo, Bo Kraven." The boy looks down at his hands when Felix laughs.

"Kraven, huh? Good name." Felix goes back to lecturing Kraven on the art of driver etiquette. The boy's smile is more thanks than Felix needs.

Felix pulls the limo into another parking lot and climbs out of the vehicle. He hands the credit card to Kraven over the top of the car. "Go get us rooms boy, the same as last time, but with a room for yourself."

Kraven takes the card and looks at Felix "I actually live not too far from here."

"Good." Felix runs a hand through his silver hair, "Get us the rooms, then go home and pack." Felix pulls an envelope out of his cost pocket and tosses it to Kraven. "You got any family here?"

Kraven nods "My parents."

Felix points to the envelope. "That envelope is your first month's wages, should be enough to keep your family comfortable. Even after you buy your new uniform."

Kraven smiles and bows to Felix, "Thank you, Master Felix." The boy turns and jogs into the hotel. Felix walks around the car to the curb side rear door. The window is open, Cassius waits for Felix to open the door, then he steps out of the car. Felix looks inside, the rest of his passengers are still dozing. Felix smiles, he takes pride in his smooth driving.

"That was great, what you did for that kid." Cassius walks with Felix to the back of the limo. With a touch from Felix's brown leather glove, the trunk unlocks and springs open.

Felix hands Cassius his backpack, then reaches to pull Viktoriya's bags from the limo. "It takes a special kind of person to do what I do." Felix lifts one of Vik's bags and his knee makes a popping sound. Felix grimaces and passes the bag to Cassius. "As you can probably tell, I'm getting too old for this kind of work. I needed someone to train so I can retire."

Cassius smiles down at the old man. "Then seeing him in a place that clearly didn't appreciate his talents had nothing to do with it?"

"Absolutely not!" Felix smiles up at Cassius, "I'm a selfish old codger who wants to spend the rest of his days drinking Irish coffee and smoking a pipe."

By this point, the rest of the passengers have stirred from their slumber. Viktoriya and Larina climb out of the limo as Kraven jogs back out of the hotel.

Kraven stops in front of Felix and Bows. "Master Felix, here are your room keys and your card."

Felix Takes the stack of plastic cards, he slides the translucent blue credit card back into his suit pocket. "Meet me back here in an hour. We have to get you your uniform, you look like a street rat."

Kraven looks at his own pressed tan slacks and white starched shirt, then he bows again. "Yes, Master Felix." Kraven spins and starts to jog out to the street, he turns onto a walking path and picks up speed.

"Kid's got hustle." Felix smiles and hands one of the clear plastic room keys to Cassius. He hands out the rest of the keys and closes the rear door of the limo. Felix turns to Vik, "I will be here tomorrow to take your friends back to the academy. I booked you this room for one week."

"Thank you, Felix." Viktoriya nods to the driver and her bows. Vik picks up her bags and turns to head into the hotel. Larina, Devirian, and Nalia follow behind Vik.

Cassius stays behind and extends his hand to the driver, "Take care of yourself, Felix."

Felix takes Cassius's hand in a firm grip. "Take care of that girl, Cassius, or you'll have her father to answer to. And he kills people for a living." Felix taps the side of his nose and smiles.

"Well, now so do I." Cassius smiles at Felix, "I'll take care of her if she'll let me."

"Best an old man can hope for I suppose." Felix walks back to the limo and climbs into the front seat. The rear window rolls up as Cassius walks into the hotel lobby. The delay meant Cassius missed the elevator. While he waits in the lobby for the next one, a heavily muscled man in a black suit jacket walks up to him.

The man speaks in hushed tones so only Cassius can hear him. "You're a fighter?" The man looks pointedly at Cassius's hand.

"Yeah, what can I do for you?" Cassius adjusts his pack on his shoulder and examines the man in the suit jacket. The man's build would lend itself to many fighting styles.

"I have been asked by the manager to remind you that we have a fully outfitted gym in the basement, as well as sparring spaces available for rental." The man smiles as Cassius.

"Thank you. You are a fighter as well?" Cassius extends his hand and the other man shakes it.

"I was." The man pulls his sleeve up. A lion's head is tattooed in red ink on the inside of his forearm. "Titus Vargas, regional champion here in New Yuma until last spring."

"Good to meet you Titus." The elevator door behind Cassius slides open and Titus nods to it.

"Best get going sir, wouldn't want to miss it again." Titus smiles and Cassius backs into the elevator.

When the elevator stops on the twelfth floor, Cassius steps off and looks at his key, the gold number suspended in the clear plastic read twelve-fourteen. Cassius walks down the hall to room fourteen, he scans the card and the mechanism in the door clicks. Cassius pushes into the room and closes the door behind him. As he walks down the short hallway created by the closet, Cassius sees Vik sitting on the second of two large beds. She has taken the bed by the window farthest from the door. When Cassius drops his bag on the bed, Vik turns to him and smiles.

"Isn't this place amazing?" Vik looks out the window, "You can see the arena from up here."

"They have a gym, and sparring spaces." Cassius says as he opens his backpack.

Vik spins around on her bed. "Seriously? Then before we do anything we have to go take a look."

"Anything?" Cassius smirks. Vik throws a shoe at Cassius, he dodges it and laughs.

Vik's wrist unit chirps, she flicks it open and reads the message on the screen. "That's Larina, she wants to go to the arena with us." Vik pulls a long grey coat out of one of her suitcases and throws it over her shoulders.

Cassius and Vik step out of their room and walk towards the elevator. Devirian is leaning against the wall in the hall across from the elevator. As Viktoriya and Cassius walk up, he closes the screen on his wrist unit and straightens up. Devi smiles at the two fighters. "Ready to go register?" Cassius and Vik both nod. "Good, everyone else is downstairs already." The elevator door opens and Devi signals for them to follow.

19

In the lobby of the hotel, Nalia is talking to Titus, while Larina scrolls through an article on her wrist unit. When the elevator doors open, both women turn. Cassius steps out of the elevator and starts to walk to the front doors, when Larina calls after him.

"Hey, do you even know where you are going?" Larina hops out of her chair and Cassius turns to took at her.

"That way?" Cassius points in the general direction of the arena. Vik and Larina both burst out laughing.

"The look on your face!" Vik laughs, she takes a deep breath and mimics the innocent look on Cassius's face. Nalia snickers at her and covers her mouth. The group gathers in the doorway and heads out into the street.

The group arrives at the arena and Nalia leads them past the box offices to a door labeled 'Coordinator'. A bald man opens the door slightly, he sees the group and opens the door farther to allow them in. Nalia steps into the room and Cassius and Vik follow her through. Devirian and Larina step to either side of the door and Larina pulls the door shut. The coordinator stumbles back to his desk.

"How can I help you?" The coordinator walks around his desk and drops into his chair.

"I'm here to register for the regional championship." Cassius drops into a seat across the desk from the coordinator. Cassius holds up his hand, revealing the snake's head tattoo.

The coordinator breathes a titanic sigh of relief. "Oh, well we can certainly get that sorted for you sir." The coordinator activates the holographic screen of his desk unit. "I'll need a name and photograph for the fight card."

Cassius flicks his wrist and the screen of a wrist unit flickers on. Daria had given the thing to him when he had signed his contract. He is still unfamiliar with the gadget, but he manages to pull up the file he is looking for and swipes it over to the coordinator's desk unit.

"Cassius Stryker, huh?" the coordinator scrolls down the fighter's identification card. "There is an account number on here, excellent." He hits a couple of keys, and a printer behind his desk starts to whir. "I'll print you a swipe card for the gym and locker rooms." The coordinator stands and offers Cassius his hand. "Welcome to New Yuma arena, Master Stryker." Cassius shakes the man's hand and sits back down.

"I am also here to register to fight." Vik steps forward and drops into the other office chair. She flicks open her wrist unit and sends her fighter's card to the Coordinator's desk unit.

The coordinator's eyes widen as he reads Vik's card. "You are the real Viktoriya Ivanov? I heard you were getting into the ring. But I never expected you to start here!" he taps a few keys and turns to the printer. He turns back when the printer stops whirring and hands both Cassius and Vik translucent gold scan cards. "These will give you access to the on-site gym, as well as the change rooms on the second floor."

Both Cassius and Vik stand, the coordinator stands as well, and offers Vik his hand. "Welcome to New Yuma, Mistress Ivanov."

Cassius and Vik thank the coordinator and, followed closely by Nalia, they walk out of the coordinator's office. Larina has moved away from the door frame and is looking at large digital posters on the far wall, she turns and calls for the rest of the group. "Your names just appeared in the ladders, guys!" Larina points up to a spot about half way down the poster where Cassius's name has appeared paired with another fighter.

"Hayden Von, huh?" Cassius fumbles his wrist unit open and jots down the name.

"Here's yours Vik." Devi points up at a bracket around six feet in the air.

"Shiori Yamada, interesting." Vik jots down the name and looks at the top of the board. "This round starts in ten days. When do you start Cass?"

Cassius looks up at the board and gulps. "These start in a week."

"Oh boy." Nalia puts her hands on her hips.

"All the more reason to party hard!" Larina throws her arm around Cassius's shoulder and starts to walk back towards the box offices.

Nalia shakes her head and follows Larina and Cassius.

"He lets you call him 'Cass'?" Devi steps up beside Viktoriya as they follow the rest of their group.

"Apparently? Maybe he just didn't notice?" Vik smiles as she walks past the box office lines. Her eye catches on a teenager in a blood-red graphic tee shirt. The logo on the shirt is a disembodied full beard wearing the world championship belt. Below that, block text reads 'RESPECT THE BEARD'. As Vik walks past she sees the back of the shirt, the back of the shirt is taken up by one word 'GIANT' Vik smiles and shouts at the teenager.

"Respect the beard!" when the teen turns around, Vik imitates her father's salute. Her fingers crook over into a tiger's paw, her thumbs reach across and touch her pinkies. The teen cheers and salutes her back. Laughing, Vik turns back to walk with Devi.

"I miss the energy of a crowd this close to a championship." Devi looks back at the lines of people waiting to purchase tickets. "It feels so alive. So many happy people."

Devi and Vik walk out of the arena and meet up with the rest of the group. Larina throws her arms into the air.

"Party time!" the short woman beams at her friends.

"Yes." Cassius nods, then he smirks at Viktoriya. "Party time indeed."

"Yeah, I still haven't looked at the gym in the hotel." Viktoriya smiles.

Cassius is standing in a dimly lit concrete hallway stretching. The roar of a crowd reverberates through the dark stone on all sides. Vik stands across from Cassius, leaning on the Concrete wall. Her face is illuminated with the soft purple light of her wrist unit.

"Let's go over this one more time." Cassius stops his stretching and starts practicing strike combinations in mid air.

Viktoriya pulls up a fighter's log for Cassius's first opponent "Hayden Von, age nineteen. Trained in striker and disrupter styles at Dragon's Breath Academy under Touma Nakamura."

"Nakamura's students always know a little bit of something that isn't registered, right?" Cassius unzips a canary yellow sweater and tosses it across the hall to Vik.

"That's right, this is his first fight out of the academy, just like you, so I don't have any rumors that might help either." Vik catches the sweater and drops it into a duffle bag on the floor. "Hair check."

Cassius sighs and pulls his ponytail out along his arm; his hair ends just before his wrist. Viktoriya nods and closes her wrist unit. "They are ready for you." Vik steps across the hall and hugs Cassius. "Come back when you're done and I'll take you for dinner."

Cassius smirks "Your treat?"

Vik slaps him in the chest, "Of course, stupid. Just come back."

"I always will." Cassius smirks and jogs off down the hall. Vik wipes her nose on her sleeve, then pulls up the live stream of the fight on her wrist unit.

"Debuting tonight from Viper's Fang Academy. Coming in at six feet four inches and two-hundred-thirty pounds, Cassius Stryker!" The man standing in the middle of the ring shouts into a microphone as Cassius jogs up the steel steps into the ring. He faces the roaring crowd and crosses his wrists under his chin, one hand covered in a navy blue fingerless glove, the other bare to show the Viper tattoo on the back of his hand. Cassius steps up beside the man in the suit. A song starts to play over the intercom system, low dulcet tones of a violin string though the arena. The man in the suit takes a deep breath and shouts into the microphone again.

"Also in his debut match tonight, from Dragon's Breath Academy. Coming in at five feet eleven inches, and one-hundred-ninety pounds, Hayden Von!" Hayden runs out and jumps into the ring. He tears his shirt from his chest to reveal a Dragon tattoo covering his entire chest.

"Because you are both new to this, let me explain the rules." A laugh goes up from the crowd as the announcer smiles. "Once that cage door closes, there are no rules!" A roar goes through the crowd and the man in the suit jogs out of the ring as the microphone rises into the air.

Hayden steps back into a low pose designed to combine the motion of slide style with the kinetic chaining of striker style. As the cage closes Cassius rushes him. Hayden sidesteps a flying knee and strikes a pressure point in Cassius's thigh. When Cassius lands, he tries to put weight on his right leg only to find it unresponsive. Cassius leans on the rubberized chain link of the cage and manages to get his leg back, but he pretends he is still debilitated. Hayden turns in a circle, basking in the roar of the crowd. When he turns back to Cassius, Hayden charges. Cassius waits for his opponent to be within striking distance then kicks out with his right leg, the strike lands on the top of Hayden's leading knee just before his weight transfers to it.

The impact makes Hayden miss his step and he stumbles right into Cassius's fist. Hayden head rocks back and he lands on the mat. Cassius drops to the mat beside Hayden, driving his forearm into his opponent's face. Hayden rolls away clutching his face. Cassius jumps to his feet and rushes at Hayden. As his opponent hauls himself to his feet, Cassius kicks him in the back of both knees. Cassius grabs Hayden by the throat and slams him into the mat. Cassius regains his feet, then drops his knee into Hayden's left elbow. The joint shatters and Hayden screams.

Cassius climbs to his feet as Hayden rolls away, he tries to use the wall of the cage to climb back to his feet. Hayden throws a desperate jab at Cassius's face. Cassius slaps Hayden's hand aside, Cassius steps through his opponent's kneecap. Cassius drops to one knee behind Hayden and pulls the man's head back over his shoulder. Cassius violently twists his shoulders and he hears a wet crunch. The bag of meat that used to be Hayden goes limp and Cassius drops the body on the mat.

Cassius stands in the center of the ring, he crosses his wrists under his chin. The cage opens and the Announcer runs up into the ring, accompanied by a mans in a long white coat. The man in the white coat kneels next to Hayden, he turns to the announcer and nods.

The announcer grabs Cassius's hand and lifts it over his head. The crowd goes crazy and Cassius smiles.

Outside the arena, Viktoriya and Cassius rush through the rain and a crowd of onlookers and reporters. One young man steps right in front of them, his press badge swings around his neck. The reporter hands Vik an umbrella and she takes it appreciatively, she opens the umbrella over her and Cassius. The reporter holds out his hand and Cassius shakes it.

"My name is Baron, I work for the New Yuma Times. You are Cassius Stryker, right?" Baron looks pointedly at Cassius's cheekbone, "He caught you a little at the end there, huh?"

Cassius smiles down at the small man "Yeah, nothing that won't heal. So, what's your deal?" Cassius looks down at the man's press badge. "Freelance, huh? That must be tough."

The shorter man looks down at his feet. "Yeah, it can be hard to get stories, especially with the new regulations." He looks back up and locks eyes with Cassius. "But that is beside the point. I would like to interview you, or at least get a few words about your fight tonight?" Baron looks expectantly at Cassius.

Cassius looks over to Viktoriya, she nods nearly imperceptibly and Cassius turns back to Baron. "We are just heading to dinner. You can join us if you like." Baron nods vigorously and follows Cassius and Vik down the street.

Outside New Yuma, in a run-down alley of the surrounding tin-town; neon lights shine out into the rain. Inside the diner, Cassius and Vik sit across from the reporter. Vik sips a steaming mug of coffee as a waitress comes to the table. The waitress sets down three plates of food with a smile and walks back into the kitchen.

Baron pulls a pad from inside his coat and sets it on the table. "So, where to start?" All through the meal Baron asks Cassius questions about his fight. When they finish eating, Baron gives Cassius a business card and disappears into the dark tin town alleys.

21

The next morning, Cassius rolls out of bed and walks into the bathroom, he looks in the mirror at the oblong patch of purple on his cheek bone. The bruise is tender and he winces when he prods it. He scrubs his hand down his stubbled face and reaches for the razor next to the sink. In a few moments, Cassius turns to get in the shower, then he sees the damage to his right thigh.

The bruise is an deep purple, almost black and about the size of his palm. Cassius whistles as he examines the injury. He prods at it with a finger and a wave of pins and needles rushes through his entire leg. Cassius climbs into the shower and turns the water on, no steam rises from the water as it pours over Cassius. In a few moments Cassius's breath is fogging and the chill water is spilling down his body, seeking out every aching muscle and calming the swelling in his leg and cheek. Cassius steps out of the shower and wraps a towel around his waist. He towels his hair until it stops dripping, then picks up a brush and walks out into the kitchen.

Cassius looks out the window in the corrugated steel wall. The view looks down a street that has a clear sight line to the arena. Cassius opens the window and a warm, dry breeze blows into the room. Cassius starts to run the steel bristled brush through his hair, Viktoriya stomps in from the next room holding a rubber spatula in one hand.

"Close the damn window. It's hot enough in here without you letting that desert wind in here." Vik stands in the doorway and crosses her arms until Cassius closes the window.

"Good morning Vik, when did you get here?" Cassius turns to face Viktoriya, her cheeks flush and she looks away.

"I came down about an hour ago." Vik tilts her head and looks at Cassius, "How's the cheek?"

"Cheek's fine. You should see my leg though." Cassius pulls his towel up to show Vik his bruise. She walks over and leans down slightly.

"That looks like it hurts." Vik jabs the bruise with her spatula and he jumps. "Go put on some pants and then come eat."

"Okay, I'll be right back." Cassius rolls his eyes and walks back into the bedroom. A few moments later, Cassius is sitting at the kitchen table. A plate of eggs and bacon sitting in front of him.

"You lived in a place like this when you were a kid?" Vik scoops eggs off her plate and shoves them in her mouth.

"Yeah, parents' place was a little bigger though." Cassius smirks at and picks up a piece of bacon. "Two bedrooms."

Vik smiles and looks at the dark steel walls, "It's just so different from what I'm used to."

"Not so different from the fighter's dorms." Cassius follows Vik's gaze to the walls. "A little darker than glass, I know. But, I can paint them if you like."

Vik Smiles, "Don't worry about that. We won't be in places like this for long."

Cassius looks down at his eggs. "Yeah, guess you're right.by the end of next week, we'll either be contenders, or we'll be dead." He looks up at Vik and smiles. "I know I'm good for it. The question is, you think you can meet me up there?"

Vik laughs, "Someone's pretty cocky."

"It's called confidence, if you could have some that would make my life easier." Cassius starts to laugh too; the pair devolve into a snickering mess.

Viktoriya recovers and clears her throat. "When is your next fight?"

"Tonight, then I'm out until finals next week." Cassius wipes up egg yolks with a heel of bread. "Then once I am the contender, I can challenge for the next three weeks, if I don't challenge for the championship by then I lose the chance and have to do it over again next season." Cassius stuffs the bread into his mouth.

"My championship chance doesn't start until after you become the contender. Can I ask you a favour?" Vik takes a sip of coffee from a ceramic mug.

"What sort of favour?" Cassius squints at Vik.

"If you can't challenge in the first three days, can you wait until after I'm a contender?" Vik looks intently into her coffee.

"What?" Cassius looks at her perplexed

"The Male Championship challenge window always occurs right on top of the Women's Qualifiers. I just want people to be able to focus on the women's competition for a while." Vik looks up at Cassius determinedly.

"You want me to challenge the Regional Champion within three days of becoming The Contender, so that people will focus on the Women's Qualifying; or more specifically, you wiping the floor with the other competitors? Okay, consider it done." Cassius smiles and stands up from the table, he takes his dishes to the sink and adds them to the pile from his mid-night snacking.

Vik laughs again. "Don't be stupid, okay?"

"Yeah don't worry. I'll be fine, I always am." Cassius walks back to the table and takes Vik's plate, he tosses it into the sink and leans on the doorframe between the kitchen and the front room. "I'm going to go for a run. Meet you back here for dinner?"

"Sure." Vik smiles and stands up. "I'm going to the gym at the arena, if your run brings you by there, drop in and say hi." Vik steps past Cassius and walks to the main door of the apartment. "See you later Cass." Vik opens the door and steps out into the hall.

"My name is Cassius." Cassius mutters to himself. He looks down at his grey cargo shorts and decides to skip the shirt today. He grabs a leather belt hanging on a chair and checks the glass bottle in one of the pouches. The bottle has been filled with powdered ice, then when the water was added, the shaved ice reformed into a single mass. By the time Cassius needs it, there will be ice cold water in the bottle. Cassius smiles and looks towards the door. He loops the belt around his waist and steps out of the apartment. Cassius steps out onto the dirt street, he starts off in a jog. He takes a turn down an alley, jumps up onto a dumpster and vaults up on top of a chain link fence. Cassius jumps to the roof of one of the apartment buildings, Cassius runs across the roofs of the uniform, steel buildings. He jumps and clears a narrow street, Cassius turns and runs the length of the next building and leaps to another. When he comes to a major road he leaps out over the street and lands on the top of a large trailer. Cassius rides the trailer for a few blocks through the tin-town. When the truck hauling the trailer pulls into the higher end buildings of New Yuma, Cassius jumps off the trailer and jogs off down a side road.

An hour later, Cassius's run does take him past the arena. He swipes his card at a door behind the box offices and jogs up the stairs. On the second level, he scans his card again, the door slides open and Cassius walks through into the men's changing rooms. He passes through and strides out into the co-ed gym space. Vik is lying on a bench pressing a three-hundred-pound bar with smooth, rapid reps. Cassius walks over and gets Vik's attention. Once she has stowed the bar, Cassius touches his still mostly frozen water bottle to Vik's inner calf. Vik's other foot snaps up and clips Cassius's chin as he steps back.

"Jerk!" Vik jumps to her feet and punches Cassius in the chest. "That sucked!"

Cassius smirks and takes a sip from the glass bottle, "Still doesn't taste right."

"It was the pewter mugs, gave the water more… Something." Vik motions for Cassius's water bottle and she takes a small sip. "Yeah, definitely the pewter mugs."

Cassius takes a moment to look at the updated ladder, his next opponent is named Kevin Grant. Cassius jots the name down in his wrist unit to look into when he gets home. Cassius jogs back down the stairs and knocks on the door to the coordinator's office. The old man opens his door and looks at Cassius.

"Ah, Master Stryker. What can I do for you today?" the coordinator, Mister Crow, opens his door and gestures Cassius into his office. Cassius sits in one of the chairs on the near side of the desk and waits for Crow to get back to his desk. Once the older man sits in his office chair Cassius leans forward. When Cassius rests his elbows on his knees Mister Crow leans forward, interlocking his fingers on his desk.

"I want an entrance track." Cassius grins roguishly.

22

Cassius and Vik are back in the dimly lit concrete hallways of the arena. Cassius hugs Vik and hands her his sweater and jogs down the hall to the arena. As he exits the concrete hallway and jogs between the stands, the crowd erupts in cheers and a kickdrum sets a hectic pace.

"Tonight, from Viper's Fang Academy. Coming in at six feet four inches and two-hundred-thirty pounds! Cassius Stryker!" the announcer hollers into his microphone. Cassius runs into the ring and jumps onto the wall of the cage. He pulls himself up and straddles the top of the cage. Cassius poses like a javelin thrower, his bronze skin making him look like a statue.

Cassius's entry track is cut short and a new sound begins. Deep bass violin sets a sense of tension. The announcer starts to shout into his microphone again. "His challenger, tonight from High Mesa Academy! Kevin Grant!" Kevin comes running in from the sidelines and steps into the ring. Cassius drops from the top of the cage, he walks over and extends his hand to Kevin. The other man grasps Cassius's forearm and both men nod. "Let's make it a good show, gents!" the announcer jogs out of the ring as his microphone rises into the air.

The cage slides shut and Kevin rushes at Cassius. The other man unleashes a spinning back kick at Cassius's face. He manages to get his guard up, but Kevin's kick still knocks Cassius to the mat. Cassius hits the mat and rolls right back to his feet. Before Kevin is able to react, Cassius slams a fist into the other man's small ribs. Kevin hunches over and Cassius Grabs him by the throat. He lifts Kevin into the air, he tries to kick free but Cassius sidesteps the kick. Using the momentum of Kevin's kick, Cassius pushes until Kevin is almost horizontal. Then Cassius slams him onto the mat, Kevin bounces off the mat and rolls onto his hands and knees. Cassius winds up to kick Kevin in the face. At the last minute, Kevin lurches up and out of the way of Cassius's foot. At the same time, Kevin's foot lashes out and catches Cassius in the back of the knee. Cassius stumbles and Kevin rushes him, Kevin bowls Cassius to the ground.

Kevin starts striking Cassius with his knees. Cassius breaks his guard, taking a knee to the side of the head but he manages to grab the back of Kevin's neck. Cassius pulls the other man over his shoulder and slams him into the mat. Cassius grabs Kevin's wrist and wrenches the joint, a wet pop signals the dislocation as Cassius jumps back to his feet. Cassius pulls Kevin into a sitting position, then kicks Kevin in the face slamming his head against the mat. Cassius backs off to let Kevin get back to his feet. When the other man doesn't move, Cassius walks over to look at Kevin. He kneels and places two fingers against Kevin's neck. Cassius frowns, then he snaps the other man's neck.

The cage opens and the announcer comes jogging into the ring. He walks up to Cassius and lifts the fighter's hand above is head. Cassius leaves the ring and jogs through the stands into the concrete back halls. When he arrives back where Vik is leaning on the wall, Cassius collapses against the cool stone wall and slides to the ground.

Vik kneels next to him. "Are you alright?" Vik snaps her fingers and holds one of Cassius's eyes open. "That knee to the head didn't do you any favours, but your brain seems to be intact. How are your ribs."

"Water, Vik. I just need some water." Cassius takes the bottle from her and gulps at it hungrily.

"Just hold still." Vik pats down his side, looking for broken ribs.

"I'm fine, promise." Cassius smiles.

"You had me worried." Vik smiles and stands up. "Let's get moving." She offers Cassius a hand up and he takes it.

Vik and Cassius hire a car back to their apartment building. A generous title for three old metal containers stacked on top of each other with stairs welded to the side. Vik helps Cassius up to the second floor. Cassius smiles and grabs the door knob.

"I got this from here. See you tomorrow morning?" Cassius turns to Vik and she hugs him.

"You did good today, Cassius. Thanks for coming back." Cassius hugs Vik back with one arm.

"Thanks, Vik. That means a lot." Cassius smirks and pushes open the door. Vik turns around and jogs up to the top floor and opens her door.

Cassius walks into his apartment and hits a light switch. Dim amber light spreads throughout the small space, Cassius looks down at his left hand, a small drop of blood is running across his palm, Cassius rubs his hand on his jeans then looks at his hand again. There is no sign of the blood on his hand. Cassius looks down at his pants, there is no stain on his jeans either. Cassius shrugs and walks into the bathroom, after a long, hot shower, Cassius collapses onto the mattress and his eyes close.

Vik wipes the floor with her opponents in the qualifying fights, becoming the regional contender with ease. The day of Cassius's title challenge, Vik walks into the coordinator's office.

"Mistress Ivanov, what can I do for you?" Mister Crow is sitting behind his desk watching an old movie.

"I want to schedule my title challenge." Vik drops into a chair on her side of the desk.

"Excellent, when will you be ready?" Mister Crow stops his movie and pulls up a calendar.

"As soon as possible, but not tonight." Vik leans in to look at the calendar.

"How about tomorrow night?" Mister Crow swipes over a square of the calendar.

"Sounds good to me, will she be in town?" Vik stands from the chair.

"Becky hasn't left since she became champion. She'll be there." Mister Crow switches the screen back to his movie. "I'll see you tonight for your friend's challenge match I assume?"

"I'll be there." Viktoriya turns and walks out of Mister Crow's office.

Cassius leans in the back hall of the arena across from Vik, just like every other fight. Vik looks up at him as he finishes his stretching.

"Are you ever going to clean that sweater?" Vik looks at Cassius's sweater. There is a small blood stain on the collar from the cut above his eye.

"It's my lucky sweater." Cassius smirks and Vik glares at him.

"It's gross." Vik wrinkles her nose as Cassius opens the sweater and drops it on the floor.

"I'll be right back." Cassius hugs Vik and jogs off down the hall.

The crowd around the ring roars as Cassius emerges from the back. His entrance track plays as he jumps into the ring and salutes the crowd. Most of the crowd copies his salute in return. Cassius's opponent is in the ring already. The Colonel, Andre Vada, is a saber fighter with striker and grappler training. Cassius takes the oak saber from the announcer and inspects it, finding it acceptable, he slides the saber into a special loop in his shorts.

Andre bows to Cassius, who returns the bow. The announcer starts the match and speed walks out of the ring. When the cage slides shut, Andre draws his saber. Cassius matches Andre's swordsmanship blow for blow, but he knows he can't keep it up for long. He charges at the champion.

Andre deflects the charge with his saber and punches Cassius in the face. Cassius over sells the impact by dropping to the mat. Andre smiles and moves to stomp on Cassius's throat. Cassius grabs Andre's foot and wrenches it to one side, throwing off the Colonel's balance. Andre catches himself with his saber, but Cassius kicks the wooden blade and Andre lands on the mat. Cassius grabs Andre's arm and swings a kick into the back of his shoulder. Andre cries out and clutches at his dislocated joint. Cassius drops an axe kick on the back of Andre's neck and the man stops moving. Cassius checks for a pulse, then snaps the champions neck.

The announcer rushes into the ring along side the medical staff. He is carrying a large belt with a plaque mounted to the front, the Regional Championship title. The announcer holds Cassius's arm up as his mic descends from the ceiling.

"Your new Regional Champion! Cassius Stryker!" Cassius's entrance track plays again and he holds the title belt over his head as the arena erupts with cheers.

Cassius walks back into the concrete tunnels and meets up with Vik, she smiles and gives him a hug. "You did it!"

"You sound surprised." Cassius smiles, "The hype was larger than the man." Cassius and Vik leave the arena through a back door and walk home along the dimly lit streets of New Yuma.

The next afternoon, Vik is sitting in Cassius's living room sipping a cup of coffee. She looks up and sees Cassius messing with his wrist unit. Cassius smiles.

"I think I'm getting the hang of this thing." Cassius taps a few more keys and the screen of the wrist unit expands into a video of his fight. "Is this how you watch me fight?"

"Usually, I don't really want to experience your death in person, you know." Vik laughs as Cassius's mouth falls open in mock betrayal.

"You don't believe in me enough to watch me die in person? For shame!" Cassius and Vik both laugh, then Vik looks down at her hands.

"I think I'm going to use Kalman tonight." Vik looks down when Cassius closes his wrist unit.

"You think you'll need it?" Cassius leans forward.

"Yeah, I think I will." Vik is till looking down when Cassius drops onto the couch beside her and puts an arm around her.

"What can I do for you?" Cassius holds her close.

"I'll need body paint, and maybe some help with my tattoo." Vik looks up as Cassius stands and walks to the door.

"Give me five minutes." Cassius is out the door before Vik can dig out her credit chip.

When Cassius gets back he and Vik head up to her apartment. Cassius helps Vik paint her shoulders and upper back in a grey black mottled pattern, then Cassius replicates Vik's Tattoo with white paint. Vik turns around and hugs him.

"I'll come get you before the fight." Cassius walks out of the apartment and locks the door behind himself. The views from Vik's floor are more open and expansive than the tight, colorful views from his own windows. Demonic music sounds from behind Vik's door as Cassius walks towards the stadium to make preparations for the fight.

When Cassius returns to collect Vik, she is unrecognizable. Her body is completely painted, even her fighting garb has been painted. Her hair has been painted black and slicked to her skull. Exaggerated eyes and mouth cover most of her face.

They enter the gym from the back, a brick Cassius had placed holds the door ajar. In the dark hallways behind the stands, Vik crouches against the wall, the mottled pattern of grey and black break up her form and making her look like nothing but a pair of floating red eyes and a massive red mouth.

In the ring, the defending women's champion, Sophie Blaze, waves to the crowd and stands next to the announcer.

"And introducing the Contender! Coming in at six foot thee inches and two-hundred pounds! The Shadow Queen, Viktoriya Ivanov!" The lights go out completely and startled a scream goes up from the crowd. In the darkness, a violin screams. When the lights come back on, Vik is standing in the ring, looking down at the champion with her exaggerated flame red eyes. The announcer rushes from the ring, the women's title belt under one arm.

The champion jumps back from Vik and puts up a high striker guard. The Shadow Queen baits a strike from Sophie and grabs her wrist. Vik pulls Sophie in and flips the smaller woman over her shoulder, she manages to tuck her head in so she isn't debilitated by landing on Vik's knee. Sophie rolls away and jumps to her feet. Vik moves fast, charging at Sophie and grabbing her by the throat. The champion strikes at Vik's side with vicious kicks, be she brushes them off and throws Sophie back into the middle of the ring. Sophie lands awkwardly, twisting her wrist on impact. Vik stalks around the champion, letting her get to her feet, she grabs Sophie's shoulder and rocks the smaller woman with a big right hook. The champion drops to the mat and Vik grabs her by the ankles. Vik starts to rotate, spinning Sophie up into the air. The crowd starts to cheer as they all recognize the signature move of Greg Ivanov, The Giant's Hammer. Vik lets Sophie fly, the crunch of bone and the squeal of metal sound in harmony as she slams into the top rail of the cage. Vik walks over and checks for a pulse, finding none, Vik walks back to the center of the ring.

Before the announcer can open the cage, Cassius steps up behind him and places a hand on his shoulder. When the man spins to look at him, Cassius just shakes his head and holds up a finger. Cassius walks up to the edge of the cage and whistles to get Vik's attention. Vik shakes her head and looks at him, she smiles and nods. Cassius turns back to the announcer and nods. The cage opens and the announcer steps into the ring and gives Viktoriya her title belt. She holds it over her head and everyone cheers. Cassius and Vik walk through the back halls of the stadium and out into the night, Vik has washed the paint off her face, hair, and hands.

Cassius's wrist unit chirps just a Vik's phone rings. Cassius looks at his wrist, a message from Daria, four words. 'We have a problem.'

Viktoriya has her phone out and answers the call.

"Hello? Yes this is Viktoriya Ivanov. What sort of bad news?" Vik's eyes tear up. "I understand, thank you." Vik throws her phone to the ground and it explodes in shards of glass and plastic.

"Hey, what happened?" Cassius puts his arm on Vik's shoulder and she leans into him.

"It's my dad..." Vik deteriorates into sobs and Cassius pulls her to him and holds her until she stops crying.

When they get back to their apartments, there is a low, black car parked out front. Kraven is leaning against the cab of the car, his suit is pristine black and a cigarette hangs from him fingers. As the pair approach, Kraven puts out the cigarette on his heel and drops it in a waste bucket on the curb.

"There has been an incident. Greg Ivanov is dead."

22

Greg The Giant sensed something was wrong the moment Stefano Bianchi walked into the ring. The man had risen through his fights almost effortlessly. Now he stands across from the Champion and smiles.

Greg blinks, and suddenly the ring has transformed into a lake of blood, his heart rate accelerates to a painful pace. Greg squeezes his eyes shut and shakes his head, when he reopens his eyes the ring is back to normal. The giant shakes his head again, he steps up to the announcer, Mister White, and the man takes hold of his wrist.

The fight starts and The Giant circles the smaller man. He baits a strike from the younger man, then grabs his arm. The Giant slams Stefano into the mat and drops on top of him. Gregg slams down on the smaller man with fists the size of sledge hammers. Stefano drops his guard and punches Greg in the ribs.

Bones crack and Greg gasps, something is wrong. Stefano punches the other side of Greg's torso, cracking more bones. Stefano slides out from under the giant and kicks the bigger man in the face, blood flies as Greg falls to the mat. Stefano jumps on top of The Giant and starts pounding on the bigger man. Within moments blood is spraying from every strike. Finally, Stefano stops his onslaught and stands up. The Cage opens and Mister White walks into the ring and gingerly reaches for Stefano's arm and raises it as the crowd boos.

Cassius stops the video. He has watched the recording more than a dozen times. "Something is very wrong with this fight." Cassius mutters to himself as he scrolls back through the video. He stops right when Stefano's first punch hits Greg. The shock in the former champion's eyes is plain. "That hit was harder than expected, huh Greg?" Cassius looks down at the autopsy paperwork he had borrowed from Vik. Not that she would notice them missing. She hadn't come out of her father's room since she had received the news.

Cassius looks at The Giant's desk. When he traveled from New Yuma with Vik, he had taken this office as his work space. He picks up the phone and dials for his fight coordinator. "Yes, Mister Crow. Thant's right, I want to register for the next World championship qualifier. Yes, I am Aware of the risk associated with a competition of this calibre. Make it happen, Mister Crow."

Cassius hangs up the phone and looks at his hands, one moment the callused skin of his hands is clean. The next moment, Blood is pouring down his wrists and dripping onto the floor. The metallic smell is over powering. Cassius squeezes his eyes shut and a moment later when he opens his eyes the blood is gone once again.

"They are getting worse, aren't they?" Vik is standing in the doorway to the office. The large white turtleneck sweater draped over her body obviously belonged to her father.

"Vik! Hey, are you feeling any better?" Cassius jumps up from behind the desk and rushes to the doorway.

"I've been better. But it was easier to get up today." Vik leans against Cassius's chest and sighs. "I just miss him."

"I know, Vik." Cassius strokes her hair. "I know." Cassius holds Vik until the phone on the desk rings. Cassius moves over to the phone and lifts the receiver. "Mister Crow, I hope you have good news?" Cassius's grins, but it looks closer to a snarl. "Thank you, sir. I'll see you in four days." Cassius hangs up the phone. "I have a match."

"How can you think about fighting right now?" Vik stares at him incredulous.

"This is what I was raised to do, Vik. It's what I know." Cassius walks towards her, but Vik pulls back.

"Don't you want to know anything else?" Vik turns and walks away from him.

Cassius supresses a wave of rage and walks back into the office. He opens his wrist unit and looks at flight schedules. He taps a button on the desk phone and a moment later, Kraven's voice comes over the intercom.

"This is Kraven."

"Hello, yes. How long does it take to get from here to the airport?" Cassius scrolls through the list of flights.

"About an hour, sir."

"Can you be ready in half that?" Cassius books a flight that leaves in two hours and rushes to the guest room where his travel bag still sits packed on the end of the bed. Cassius stops outside Vik's father's room. He knocks on the door frame and pokes his head through the open door.

"What are you doing?" Vik calls to him from downstairs. The supersized sweater is still in place, but Vik has slung a large duffle bag over one shoulder. Her hair is contained under a ball cap, and her wrist unit screen is shining with the same list of flights Cassius had been looking at.

Cassius smiles. "What's up, Vik?" he jogs down the stairs and starts to walk towards the front door.

"Where are we going? I assume you didn't book me a seat?" Vik catches up and starts to scroll through the flight schedule.

"We?" Cassius stops and looks at Vik, "What happened to you wanting me to quit?"

"I realized that, if you went off and got yourself killed without me, I wouldn't be able to forgive myself." Vik smiles "Besides, someone has to be there to patch you up."

"I'm on the flight to Rome in two hours." Cassius starts to walk towards the door again. Vik is still standing where he left her.

"Rome?" Vik asks in a low voice.

"Yeah, like I said. 'I have a match.'" Cassius opens the front door of the Ivanov house and tosses his duffle bag to Kraven.

Viktoriya storms out of the door and jumps into car across from Cassius. "Rome? You are going after Stefano Bianchi?"

"I Can beat him, Vik. I know I can."

Vik starts to tear up. "My father was the greatest fighter in history and that monster killed him. What makes you think he'll do any different to you?"

"Your father didn't know Stefano was cheating!" Cassius shouts and Vik's eyes flare. "He was hitting harder than he should be able to, your father didn't realize it until it was too late."

"We have to report him." Vik flicks open her wrist unit and starts to hit keys.

"No!" Cassius reaches across and closes the screen of her wrist unit. "Just hear me out, okay?" Cassius raises his hands as Viktoriya glares at him. "You report him, and if anyone looks into it, he gets disqualified. But then I can't do anything about it. At least if he is the champion, I can make him pay."

Vik smirks and reopens her wrist unit. "I see." She closes the complaint form and turns the screen back off. She climbs into the back seat of the car and Cassius follows.

"Thank you, Vik." Cassius sits back as Kraven closes the passenger door and walks around to the driver's seat.

When Vik and Cassius arrive in Rome, they make their way to the arena. The sign above the entrance to the massive stadium reads "New Coliseum Arena."

"Mister Crow said he couldn't get me a match. How can the previous National Coordinator not get me a match?" Cassius walks around to the side of the box office. Two large fighters step up and block his way, one of them points to a plaque mounted on the wall that reads "Employees Only" Vik touches Cassius on the wrist and he steps back and takes Vik's duffle bag.

"Hello, gents." Vik smiles charmingly "This is Cassius striker, and I'm his manager Viktoriya Ivanov." The guard's eyes widen and Vik drops the affectation. "Yeah, you heard me, Ivanov. The reign of The Giant may be over, but it is not too late for retribution. We need to see a coordinator, immediately."

"That won't be necessary, Mistress Ivanov." Cassius spins to see a darks skinned man in a white suit walking towards them. The man leans on a cane and rises a hand to the two fighters blocking the doorway.

"It's all right boys." He limps forward on his cane and pats one of the fighters on the shoulder. Then he turns to Vik.

"Your fighter can wait out there. Please follow me." He walks past his guards and into an office.

Cassius drops onto a concrete bench and stares at the two fighters guarding the door. A short while later, Vik emerges from the office with a navy-blue translucent swipe card on a lanyard. She smiles at the guards and gives Cassius a thumbs-up. Cassius stands up with both of their duffle bags over his shoulder. Vik hold the swipe card up for him to see.

"Okay, you're in. It was a tough sell, I might have… exaggerated your accomplishments a tad. But you have the fight you wanted. Two days, he's a Grecian. They call him 'The Nemean Lion' they say he has never bled in the ring. That's a streak I know you can break."

Cassius smiles "So, about finding a place to stay?" he flips open his wrist unit while he waits for a taxi.

"Actually, Cassius…" Vik is standing next to a low black saloon car, the door opens and Felix steps out of the cab of the car. "I have a place already."

Cassius nods his head at Felix, "I thought they retired you, Felix. How are you?"

"I'm cursed to work for these people until I die, they just relocated me somewhere prettier to do it." Felix grins and waves Cassius over. "Get in, kid."

A few miles away from the arena, Felix pulls into an underground parkade filled with cars. They range from the newest designs, to iconic early models. Every car is painted in a shade of black or grey. When Cassius climbs out of the car he notices an archway into another section of the parkade. The area past the arch contains the gems of the collection. Antique diesel and petroleum powered cars. The vibrancy of the paint on these pieces of automotive art make allowances for the drab nature of the surrounding collection.

"Do you like them?" Felix walks up behind Cassius with a smile. "They were Master Ivanov's favorites." He points to a sleek, low sitting machine, "He left that to me. But I can't afford to even start the thing, not on my current salary anyway." He laughs.

Felix leads Vik and Cassius upstairs into a well-appointed home. He takes them to a pair of bedrooms on the upper floor. "Let me know if you need anything else. I'll be around." Felix turns around and walks back down the stairs.

"I'm going for a run." Cassius tosses his duffle bag into one of the spare rooms.

"Care for some company?" Vik tosses her bag as well and stretches.

"You think you can keep up?" Cassius turns and vaults over the railing behind him. Dropping to the main floor, Cassius races for the front door, Vik jumps down after him and gives chase. When Cassius looks back, she is smiling again.

The night of Cassius's fight, he and Vik are sitting in the gym at the stadium. Cassius is wrapping up his warm up while Vik quizzes him on his opponent.

"Stelios Terzi, The Nemean Lion, his style is a combination of slide and striker styles. The rumor is that he has never bled in the ring.

He is the current favourite with all the bookies who would talk to me." Vik scrolls down the screen of her wrist unit.

"Can I use a saber?" Cassius stands up from the bench and rolls his neck.

Viktoriya smiles. "You want to make sure he bleeds."

"If he bleeds, he is human. If he is human, I can beat him." Cassius unzips his hoodie, the once bright yellow garment is now faded and stained with sweat and blood spots. "It's time."

Vik stands up from her bench and takes Cassius's face in her hands. "Come back, okay?" Vik kisses Cassius, then she pulls back and smiles.

"You haven't done that since the academy. You are really worried, huh?" Cassius hugs Vik and holds her close. "I'll come back. I always have, haven't I?"

"You have, you're right." Vik looks into his eyes, "Just let me be concerned."

Cassius smiles and kisses Vik on the forehead, then he turns and jogs from the gym.

A narrow bridge connects the edge of the ring to a tunnel under the stands. Cassius's entrance track starts and he strides up to the ring. He walks up to Mister White and stands next to him. A few seconds later, a lion's roar starts a second entrance theme and The Nemean Lion jogs across the bridge and into the ring. He is older than Cassius by about five years, and his skin is flawless. Cassius can't see a single scar. Cassius slides the solid oak saber into a loop on his shorts and bows to Terzi, the older man bows in turn.

Mister White sets the match and jogs out of the ring. As the cage slides shut Terzi growls at Cassius. "You think you can kill The Nemean Lion? You are just a boy, I will chew you up and spit you back at whatever academy trained you."

"I may be just a kid, but so was Hercules." The cage door closes with a metallic click and Cassius moves like lightning. Drawing his wooden saber, Cassius feigns a big overhead swing, when Terzi side steps to avoid it, Cassius uses the momentum of the swing to kick his back leg up. As Cassius is turned by the momentum of his swing, his foot connects unexpectedly with Terzi's face. The Lion is rocked by the blow and staggers backwards. Cassius swings the sabre and connects with the side of Terzi's knee. The joint collapses under the pressure and The Lion drops to the ground, dazed. Cassius drops the saber and rushes Terzi he launches a flying knee at the man's face, but Terzi manages to roll out of the way to avoid the blow. Using his good leg, The lion snaps a kick into Cassius's gut. When Cassius hunches from the strike, Terzi grabs a handful of his hair.

Cassius's eyes flash and he grabs Terzi's wrist, with a violent twist Cassius breaks The Nemean Lion's wrist. Using the broken joint as leverage, Cassius drives a forearm strike into Terzi's elbow. The joint snaps and bends backwards as Cassius drives his knee into the other man's face. A spray of blood erupts from The Nemean Lion's nose as his head rocks back. Cassius releases his arm and lets the man fall back to the mat, when he looks down at his hands, small flecks of blood have splattered his palms. He wipes the blood onto his shorts and looks down at the man lying on the mat. The jeers of the crowd wash over him and Terzi chokes on his own blood. Cassius stomps on The Nemean lion, his heel crushing the other man's skull. When the Cage opens, Mister White rushes in from the sidelines and lifts Cassius's arm in the air.

"Your winner, and the new World contender. Cassius Stryker!" the cheer from the crowd is intoxicating as Cassius crosses the bridge from the ring and disappears back behind the stands.

Vik is waiting in the hall, she is wearing Cassius's sweater. He smiles at her, but she points to where a woman in a white lab coat is standing next to a gurney. Cassius rolls his eyes and walks over; the woman pats the gurney and Cassius climbs up and sits on the thin mattress. The doctor takes a pair of stainless steel pliers from a tray and looks at Cassius's knee. She wipes blood away with a damp cloth, then grabs something with the pliers. Cassius flinches as she pulls what looks like a tooth from the skin above his knee. She pours peroxide on Cassius's leg, the liquid foams as it runs down and he winces as the doctor grabs another tooth and yanks it free. She sets the pliers back on the tray and pours more peroxide on his leg. Next, she picks up a needle and a spool of blue medical thread. The doctor looks at Cassius with the usual question in her eyes. Cassius shakes his head, no need for numbing. The doctor nods and quickly puts a single stitch in each wound, sealing them shut. She then wraps Cassius's knee in gauze and an elastic bandage.

Cassius thanks the Doctor and stands from the gurney. He walks over to Viktoriya and she hugs him gingerly.

"Thanks, my ribs are going to be sore." Cassius smiles at Vik and she kisses him again. "Okay, hold up." Cassius touches his hand to Vik's forehead. "Are you feeling okay?"

"I'm better than okay." Vik smacks his hand away and smiles. "Let's get going, you need to rest up before your next fight."

Cassius smiles and follows Viktoriya to a back door out of the arena. A car is waiting in the alley. Felix is leaning on the car, a pipe in one hand. He is watching a recording of the fight on his wrist unit. When Vik and Cassius approach, Felix beams at the pair and taps out his pipe.

"Well done, Cassius." Felix extends his hand and Cassius shakes it.

"Thank you, Felix." Cassius lets Felix open the door then he slides into the back of the car. Vik drops in next to him and the door closes. Felix climbs down into the cab then navigates the car through the back alleys.

As Vik and Cassius climb the stairs in Felix's home, Cassius freezes at the top of the stairs. He looks down at his hands; blood is pooling in his palms and pouring down his arms. As he looks around the floor is covered in a pool of blood. The stairs have transformed into a crimson waterfall. Cassius gasps and falls to one knee, Vik turns back and her eyes widen, she kneels in front of Cassius and cups his face in her hands.

"Hey, you going to be okay?" Vik locks eye with Cassius and his breathing slows.

"Yeah." Cassius climbs back to his feet and rubs his hands together. The blood is gone, but his hands still tingle. "Yeah, I'll be fine."

"Get some rest. You need to let yourself heal." Vik helps Cassius to his bed and smiles.

Cassius wakes the next morning to see Vik lying on the other side of his bed. She must have come back in during the night. Cassius lies back down and closes his eyes, better to let her sleep than to risk disturbing her.

24

"Two days is not long enough for my fighter to heal properly! Of course, I'm more than a little angry!" Vik shouts into the phone while she paces on a rooftop, sixty feet in the air. "What do you mean 'We are on a tight schedule?' This is the world bloody championship we are talking about here!" She pulls her phone away from her ear and gives it the finger. Cassius stifles a laugh as Vik puts the phone back to her ear. "You know what? Are you in your office right now? I'll be there in six minutes." Vik ends the call and looks over to Cassius, "How was that?"

"Convincing." Cassius smiles and nods in the direction of the arena. "Race you?"

"You're on." Vik sprints and leaps from the edge of the rooftop. She lands on the rooftop of a lower building and rolls. Popping back to her feet she looks around, then starts to run. Cassius smiles and follows her lead. His knee is still a little stiff, but the wounds in his skin have completely healed.

Vik's meeting goes exactly how she had planned. Her request to have the fight delayed was thrown out, and doubts about Cassius's ability to fight in title match have started to circulate. She decides to meet Cassius back at the house and takes a walk through the ancient city. When she arrives home, Cassius is lounging on a couch. She smiles and walks over to sit with him. The television in the room is on, Cassius is watching a livestream of the women's qualifier in New Yuma.

"Your defence is coming up soon." Cassius sits up as Vik walks into the room. "You do so much to help me win. I figured the least I could do is keep an eye on your possible opponents."

Vik smiles "Thank you. It means a lot." Viktoriya sits down on the couch next to Cassius and the pair pass the day making strategies any analyzing fighters. Felix walks past and sees the two completely absorbed in the program and their conversation. A few minutes later he walks into the room with two large, flat boxes.

"The night before every title match, Master Ivanov would order a large pizza from Giovani's just down the road. He used to say, 'If I die, I don't want to regret my last day.' Giovani's is the only place in all of Rome that still uses meat that isn't lab grown." Felix set the pizza pies down on the coffee table. "I'll be around if you need anything." Felix turns to leave but Cassius sits up.

"Felix, these smell really good, thank you." Cassius inhales exaggeratedly though his nose. "Would you like to join us for dinner?"

Felix smiles "Thank you for the offer Cassius, but I've already eaten."

Vik looks up as well, "Would you like to watch these fights with us then?"

The old driver laughs, "Again, thank you Mistress Viktoriya. But I watched enough fights with your father to know not to watch a fight with a fighter." He points at the screen, "For example, how long has that poor girl been upside down for?" Cassius laughs and Felix smiles.

"Thank you again, Felix." Cassius bows slightly to the old man. Felix bows and wanders off.

"I don't want to regret my last day, huh?" Cassius looks at the pizzas, "Your dad was brilliant, Vik."

"Yeah." Vik wipes her eyes and sniffles. Cassius reaches around her shoulders and pulls her against his side.

"It's going to be okay." Cassius kisses Vik on the top of the head. She nods then reaches for a pizza box.

"Do you want to just watch these all the way through the first time?" Vik opens the pizza box and the smell of real, fried meat hits the two like a sledgehammer.

"Sure." Cassius takes a slice of pizza and starts the fight again. As the fight continues, Cassius looks over at Vik. She is smiling and eating pizza, but he can tell she is still tense.

Stefano steps out of the back hallway and into the ring. Hundreds of people boo as he poses next to Mister White.

Mister White taps a pin in his coat lapel and his voice booms out across the stadium, "And introducing our challenger, from New Yuma. Cassius Stryker!" Cassius's entrance track starts to play, the haunting violin singing over the crowd. The entire the stadium sits in tense silence, waiting to see if Cassius will return.

Then he emerges from behind the stands and the crowd erupts in uproarious cheers. Cassius steps into the ring and salutes the crowd, crossing his wrists under his chin. Many people copy his salute.

A chant starts low and builds 'Saber! Striker! Grappler! Breaker!'

Eventually the chant dies and Cassius takes his place next to Mister White. The announcer starts the match and jogs for the edge of the ring.

Before the cage slides closed, the world champion moves. His first strike almost catches Cassius off guard and he barely manages to avoid the swing. Cassius recovers quickly, he lashes out at Stefano with a jab to the ribs. Stefano grunts then swings again, Cassius deflects the strike and retaliates with a headbutt. Stefano's nose explodes with blood as he staggers back.

Cassius glances down at his hands, small pools of blood are starting to form in his palms, he wipes his hands on his shorts and charges at Stefano. The world champion throws a wild punch that catches Cassius in the side. Even though Cassius had mentally prepared for the impact, the incredible force behind the strike still takes him off guard. Cassius feels his ribs crack and he lands on the mat. When his eyes refocus, the ring is covered in blood, his hands are pouring blood, forever stained by it. Stefano kicks Cassius in the stomach and he coughs blood. As Cassius's blood drops into the pool in his vision ripples travel all the way to the edge of the ring. Then Cassius sees Viktoriya. She is standing in the low space around the ring, her eyes are wide in fear.

Cassius squeezes his eyes shut. When he opens them again the pools of blood are gone. Cassius grabs Stefano's next kick and twists his ankle. The champion lets out a cry and falls to the mat. Still controlling him by his ankle, Cassius drags Stefano into the middle of the ring. Cassius lets his ankle go and the champion scrabbles to his knees. Stefano throws another punch and Cassius grabs his wrist. He drives his thumb into a pressure point and Stefano's hand pops open. Cassius drives an elbow strike through Stefano's fingers. The champion screams and Cassius releases his hand and it falls to the mat. Cassius winds up and kicks Stefano in the face. The other man's neck snaps and his body falls to the mat. Blood pours from his hand where shining metal has torn through the skin.

"I knew you were cheating you monster." Cassius touches the side of his chest and feels his ribs, one is broken. Two more are bruised or cracked. The cage opens and Mister White walks into the cage and steps around Stefano's body. He hands Cassius a large belt with an ornate looking central plaque. Cassius throws the belt over his shoulder and lets Mister White lift his arm over his head.

"Your new World Champion, Cassius Stryker!" the crowd cheers and chants. Cassius salutes the crowd one more time and walks from the ring. Vik intercepts him in the hall and gives him a hug.

"Ow, damn it Vik, my ribs!" Vik jumps back and looks at Cassius's ide, the deep purple of broken bones is barely visible under his bronze skin. When Vik looks up Cassius is smiling. "I told you, didn't I? I told you I would come back."

Vik tears up, "Yeah, you might have mentioned that." Cassius leans in and Kisses her.

Made in the USA
San Bernardino, CA
21 December 2017